Also by Gregoı

The Wright Cousin Adventures

The Treasure of the Lost Mine

Desert Jeepers

The Secret of the Lost City

The Case of the Missing Princess

Secret Agents Don't Like Broccoli

The Great Submarine Adventure

Take to the Skies

The Wright Cousins Fly Again

Reach for the Stars

The Sword of Sutherlee

The Secret of Trifid Castle

The Clue in the Missing Plane

Additional Books

Rheebakken 2: Last Stand for Freedom

Strength of the Mountains

The Hat, George Washington, and Me!

"So, Jonathan, what do you think of our new book cover?" asked Kimberly. "It's a night picture of the George Washington Memorial in Washington, D.C."

"Looks good," said Jonathan.

"I did see Tim with a pair of scissors, a piece of white paper, and some markers," Kimberly said. "You don't think he's planning on doing anything to the cover this time, do you? And we keep finding those smiley faces hidden on our front covers."

"Tim? No, he's probably just prepping for his spelling test. He even asked me how to spell the word *SPIES*."

Secret Agents Don't Like Broccoli

SECRET AGENTS DON'T LIKE BROCCOLI

Gregory O. Smith

Visit **GregoryOSmith.com**

Author's Note

The Wright cousins become secret agents? No way! And then, suddenly, there they are in the thick of it, doing what the Wright cousins do best, turning the international spy world upside-down with totally amazing panic and confusion. Grab your trench coat, hat, and sunglasses, and watch out for bad guys as you join the Wright cousins to find out why *SECRET AGENTS DON'T LIKE BROCCOLI*

CHAPTER 1

Spies!

If I had not been there, I would not have believed it myself. But here's how it went...

The news spread incredibly fast: **PRINCESS KATRINA MISSING! FEARED KIDNAPPED BY SPIES!**

Deep within the U.S. White House, a national security meeting was now in progress. Using ultra-scrambled fiber optic links, the President of the United States was on the phone. From his manner, it was obvious to all present that he was *not* in a good mood. "I don't care what's going on in the Middle East right now," the President said seriously. "This is a Top Secret, Priority One Alpha Mission. I want our best agents on it!"

On the other end of the line was the frazzled director of the American Secret Intelligence Agency–the SIA–listening. "We have a slight problem, Mr. President, sir," replied the SIA man. "Search Team Beta isn't scheduled for active duty yet."

"I don't want problems, Mitchell," replied the President

urgently. "I want answers. If you had listened to me in the first place, we wouldn't be in this predicament. Forget the Beta unit and find your top two agents. I know she's not an American citizen, but I want Princess Katrina Straunsee and that top secret attaché case found, *now!* And while you're at it, get Delta Forces out there. This could mean war!"

Mitchell, his short gray hair standing on end, winced as the President slammed down his phone receiver. "Yes sir, Mr. President, sir," Mitchell said belatedly. Recently appointed to head the SIA, Mitchell was not enjoying his new assignment. He turned to his aide. "Ralph, you heard the president. He wants our top agents on this job. Who have we got?"

"I'll check," said Ralph, quickly speaking into his computer.

"We need the best," added Mitchell. "Someone we can trust to not mess this thing up."

"Top secret agents coming up now, sir," said Ralph, still glancing at his computer.

* * *

Hundreds of miles away, two unsuspecting cousins were also very busy.

"Hey Robert, watch this," called out fourteen-year-old Tim Wright to his cousin. They were playing frisbee on the front lawn of Robert's house. Leaping into the air, Tim spun around and launched his frisbee toward Robert. The frisbee flew high over Robert's head and lodged in the branches of a tall pine tree.

"Better stick to pizza crusts," Robert laughed as he turned to retrieve the frisbee. Hearing his watch beep, Robert called out, "Timbo, you'll have to get it. Somebody's trying to reach me again."

A month before, Robert had linked his wristwatch alarm into his computer email system. From the number of false alarms he'd gotten in the last fifteen minutes, he was beginning to think it was a mistake.

"Just ignore it," Tim called back. "It's probably just Lindy again."

Lindy, Robert's twin sister, had been trying to email him something all morning, but fearing it might be a list of chores, Robert hadn't stopped to read it. Curious, Robert jogged into the family room to check on the source of the new message. He was expecting some research data for a huge semester project due in two weeks. Robert was very anxious to get the data retrieved and locked down safely on his hard drive.

Tim, meanwhile, had shinnied up the tree after the frisbee. Hugging the trunk, he reached for a higher branch. Grabbing that, he swung himself up still higher. He was hanging upside-down by his knees when Robert returned from the house.

"Hey Tarzan," Robert called out. "It was from Kimberly. She says it's time to come home—*right away.*"

Kimberly was Tim's blonde-haired, older sister. Early on, Kimberly had taken it upon herself to make sure Tim survived beyond his youth. Knowing Tim, it would not be an easy task.

Tim grabbed the frisbee and sent it gliding smoothly down toward Robert. "Did she say why?" Tim asked, hanging by his left hand.

"No," Robert called back. "Just some sort of emergency or something."

"She probably just needs help on her Algebra 2 again," Tim replied with a grin.

Robert laughed. Of the five Wright cousins, Kimberly was the second best mathematician. And, Tim, well, he barely survived the subject. Robert felt his wristwatch beep again and headed back into the house. This time, Tim dropped from the tree and trotted in after him.

"Wow," said Tim as they entered Robert's room, "you do have carpet in your room."

"No thanks to you," Robert replied, shaking his head. "You and your potato chip fight ideas. Do you know how long it took me to get all those chips off the floor?"

Tim grinned sheepishly. "You've got to admit, though, it *was* more fun than a pillow fight."

"Tell that to the vacuum," said Robert, pressing a remote control button on his watch.

Across the room, the screen on his computer flickered to life. "All right!" said Robert, spotting a new icon in the upper right-hand corner of the screen. "My research program finally got through."

Pulling out a desk chair, Robert plunked down in front of his computer and swung out the keyboard. He clicked on the new icon.

"Enter username," appeared on the screen.

"Kimosoggy," Robert typed in.

"Library Data File: Enter City Please–."

"Toronto," replied Robert.

"There's a city named Toronto?" asked Tim.

"Sure," said Robert. "Don't you remember? Great-Grandpa used to live there. Toronto, Canada. Here, watch this."

Robert clicked on the word *Toronto* and a topographic map appeared on the screen. Selecting an airplane icon from the side of the screen, the city suddenly took on a three-dimensional appearance as if viewed from a low flying airplane.

"Wow," said Tim. "That's a great program."

"And watch this," said Robert, dumping his airplane icon for one in the shape of a car. The screen changed. They were now driving through the streets of downtown Toronto. It was so detailed they could even see the cracks in the pavement.

* * *

"Who have we got?" asked SIA Chief Mitchell, back in Washington, D.C.

"Coming up on the screen now, sir," said Ralph. "I had to use our Alpha clearance to run the search. Chief, these two guys are so secret that they're known only by their code names."

"I see," said Mitchell, growing more impatient by the minute. "And what are their code names?"

Ralph glanced at the screen and then back at his boss. "Code names..." The screen flickered off for a second and back on again. "*Kimosoggy and Toronto.*"

"Who?" asked Mitchell.

"Kimosoggy and Toronto, sir."

"Kimosoggy and who?" Mitchell said, suddenly looking as if he'd swallowed his necktie.

"Kimosoggy and *whom*, sir. *Whom* is the proper word." Mitchell's face turned bright red and Ralph looked at him worriedly. "It's your blood pressure again, sir, isn't it?"

"Kimosoggy and *whom?*" blurted out Mitchell in exasperation.

"Oh, Toronto, sir. Kimosoggy and Toronto. They're the best. I mean, they must be, because that's who our computer came up with. Only we haven't been able to make contact with them for a while. I think they're on vacation."

"Vacation?" Mr. Mitchell just about fainted. "Ralph, find this Kimosoggy and Toronto team and get them moving. Don't eat, don't sleep until they've found Princess Straunsee and that attaché case!"

Unbeknownst to Mr. Mitchell and Ralph, there was a hidden listening device—a "bug"—in the room. The bug picked up the new agent names and the spy world suddenly went crazy. Every foreign embassy in Washington, D.C., was a-buzz with urgent orders to find the two American agents, Kimosoggy and Toronto; some to help them, others to bury them.

"Yavohwl!" commanded the Germans. "Zwei agent Amerikaner! Kimosoggie und Toronto. Schnell!"

"Da!" shouted the Russians. "Dva angliskee. Keemosoggee eee Toronto."

The Chinese: "Wahn-AHN. Ching, ar foo-chin. Kimosoggy, Toronto."

No matter what the language, the whole spy world was suddenly out to get America's top two secret agents, and only two people knew where they were—Kimosoggy and Toronto—*and they weren't telling!*

CHAPTER 2

Trouble in Toronto

They weren't telling because not even *they* knew who they were.

"Try flying the helicopter," said Tim. Robert switched to the helicopter and soon they were flying a virtual helicopter on the computer screen—no more than fifty feet above the ground—through a maze of skyscrapers.

"Boy, this would make a great video game," said Tim excitedly. "Wish I had to do a term paper like this. Hey, look out for that building!"

Moving his joystick to the left, Robert swerved to miss the building. Too late, the helicopter's rotors hit a pillar and swung the nimble craft into a large fifth-story office window. With a loud crash, the helicopter flipped on its side and spun around into a large indoor water fountain. Then the computer screen went blank.

"You crashed it extra good," said Tim with admiration. "Let me try it now."

"That and my computer," said Robert, only half listening. "I knew I should have saved it to hard drive before we tried it. Those temporary files are always giving me problems."

Robert tried punching in some commands, but his computer would not respond and the screen remained black. "Great, just great. If I don't get it back, I'm gonna get creamed in Mrs. Barnstorm's history class." Robert was about to push the reset button when a question flashed across the screen:

"Access Toronto?" it said.

Taking a deep breath, Robert carefully typed in "yes."

"Toronto?" appeared again on the screen. "Kimosoggy and Toronto." The computer beeped twice and the word "Cleared" appeared on the now green screen.

"Thank goodness," said Robert, finally exhaling.

"Press *ENTER* to access Toronto." Robert did.

"Go with Toronto," said the computer. "Priority 1 Clearance, ALPHA COMMAND. Begin download. Now!"

"Greetings, Kimosoggy and Toronto. Prepare for a message from the President."

Robert's laser printer immediately clicked on and started printing out words so fast he had to grab hold of it to keep it from bouncing off the shelf. With a *Zip!* the printer finished its page and sent it sailing out into the middle of the room.

"Whoa," said Robert. "Somebody's got some heavy-duty software."

Tim scooped up the paper. "Hey, listen to this," he said. "General Kimosoggy, years ago you served our country during the Ice Cream Cone Wars..."

"Give me that, you big spoofer," said Robert, grabbing it out of his hands. Robert glanced at the paper:

TOP PRIORITY ALPHA COMMAND: MEMORIZE AND DESTROY. LOCATE KATRINA STRAUNSEE, ATTACHÉ AT ALL COSTS. DELTA STAR 246~RES: SMITH & JONES.

DEST: PORT A, LOCK 9257. WES-SAV 107345000-3291 UNCLOSED CL ON INQUIRY

What's that supposed to mean?" asked Tim, looking over Robert's shoulder.

"Delta Star," said Robert. "*Delta*..." The puzzled look on his face quickly changed to a knowing grin. "Goofer Mike, that's who sent it. He almost got me that time."

"Who?"

"You remember Mike Jones–Goofer Mike–that used to live here until he moved to Washington, D.C., last winter? Ever since I beat him at Internet chess, he's been trying to get revenge. The *Delta Star* part gave it away, though, he's always saying *Delta* this and *Delta* that. He thinks he's some big secret agent or something."

Robert's computer monitor beeped again. The word "Acknowledge" appeared on the screen.

"Sure," Robert grinned, going along with the gag, and typed in: "Yes sir, over and out. 10-4, good buddy, don't get your feet wet, and may the force be with you."

Robert was planning his next move to outsmart his friend when the phone rang in the kitchen. Tapping a button on his watch, Robert transferred the call over to his computer.

"Hello?" said a familiar female voice over the computer's speakers.

"Hi, Kimberly," said Robert. "How's my favorite cousin?"

"Flattery will get you nowhere, Robert," said Kimberly. "Where's my brother, Tim?"

Robert motioned for Tim to scram. "Tim? Yeah, he was over here this morning."

"Is he still there?" asked Kimberly.

"Who?"

"Tim. You know, my irresponsible younger brother who told Mom he'd have the dishes put away before she got back home this morning."

"Don't worry, Kimberly," said Robert, still stalling for time. "I'm sure your good, extremely responsible younger brother is on his way home right now," Robert replied. "Out."

Tim ran all four blocks to his home. When he got there, he met Kimberly just heading out the front door.

"Forget the dishes," Kimberly said matter-of-factly, "I already put them away."

"Then why did you call me home?" asked Tim.

"For another reason," said Kimberly. "Tim, when are you going to start being more responsible. People depend on you, you know, like Mom. And I can't always cover for you. It's just not right."

"I know," said Tim uncomfortably. "It's just that, well, you're so *good* at doing the dishes and *enjoy* doing them so much–."

"Nice try," Kimberly said. "You're in deep trouble now."

"I didn't do it," said Tim. "Honest."

"Yes, you did," Kimberly shot back. "Here's the proof."

Tim hadn't noticed it before, but Kimberly was holding a piece of paper which she now shoved into his hand. "Report cards already?" Tim asked apprehensively, trying to give it back to her.

"No, you lucky goose," Kimberly said, hardly able to contain her excitement. "It's from the PoemNet people. And Tim, you're not going to believe it. Remember that poem you wrote? I sent it in for you—and guess what—*you won!*"

CHAPTER 3

Teenage Genius

"I did?" said Tim. "With that crazy poem I made up?"

Kimberly glanced back down at the paper and read the poem aloud:

KNIGHT AND DAY
by Timothy Wright, Esquire, Poet-at-large

I saw a knight named Day,
the trees are leaving, April, May.
Airplanes fly, thinking soundly,
moon defies view, looking roundly.
Ground watch, rooks, many pawns;
start sprinklers, water lawns.
There, because.

"That thing won?" said Tim in disbelief.

"And listen to this," said Kimberly. "The writer of this breathtakingly beautiful poem is hereby notified that he is the sole winner and Grand Champion of the PoemNet Poetry Contest. Furthermore, he is hereby invited to produce a reading of his poem before the International Poets and Whizbanger Society, complete with round-trip, all expenses paid to Washington, D.C., for himself and his family."

"And look at this," said Kimberly, handing him a second page from the Internet. "Your poem is already getting some national reviews."

Tim's jaw dropped as he read them. "**TEENAGE POET GENIUS TO TOUR EAST COAST!**" one headline announced. "**Profound**," says *U.S.A. Tomorrow*. "**Deeply significant**," says the *Washington Toast*. "**A must-read poem**," pronounced *The Wallet Street Journal*. "**How did we ever live without it?**" queried *The New York Rhymes*. "***KNIGHT AND DAY*** **TAKES LITERARY WORLD BY STORM!**"

CHAPTER 4

Great Aunt Opal

You'd never believe how many emails and telephone calls Tim got. Why, he was downright famous. People asked his advice on all sorts of matters, wanting him to speak at this or that meeting. There was the "First Annual National Fun 'Hey, Pay-Attention-To-Me' March," now in its fifth year, the International Poet Postulators wanted a reading, and the Governor of the state even wanted him to address the state legislature to help the cause of education.

It came as a huge surprise to Kimberly and Tim's mom as well. "Tell me again," she said. "Tim won the PoemNet

Contest and they're paying our way to go to Washington, D.C.?"

"Yes," said Kimberly. "But we have to leave by tomorrow morning. They want Tim to give his poem reading tomorrow night at the 145th International Poets and Whizbanger Society meeting in Washington, D.C. And we have a paid vacation for a whole week to tour all the monuments and museums there. Oh Mom, isn't it great? Do you think we can make it?"

Kimberly suddenly remembered her older brother's condition. "Oh Mom," she added, "do you think you and Jonathan will be able to come?"

Jonathan, age 18, was Kimberly and Tim's oldest brother and the oldest of the Wright Cousins. Planning on majoring in Electrical Engineering at college, he worked an after-school job flipping burgers at Radio Snack, the restaurant that offers "A *bit in every byte.*" A few days before, he had accidentally slipped on a grease spill and hit his head on the hard concrete floor. At the hospital, they found he had a slight concussion. He was now home, resting under his mom's watchful care.

"I need to stay with Jonathan," said Mrs. Wright.

Mrs. Wright had a real understanding of medical problems. Her husband called it "Mom's gift of intuitive discernment." Though Kimberly and Tim were disappointed, deep down they knew where their mom needed to be.

Mrs. Wright smiled proudly at Kimberly and Tim. "You two are incredible!" she said. "Now, you'd better hurry and get packed and I'll–." She paused, looking at Tim. "I'd better see if great Aunt Opal can go along as your *chaperone*."

"Aw, Mom, *not her*," said Tim. "Aunt Opal's always picking on me. She makes me tuck in my shirts all the time and keep my shoes tied."

"That's good," replied his mom.

"But she makes me re-tie them every five minutes, whether

they need it or not. It's wearing out my shoelaces. And besides that, she always brings us her cooked broccoli things for dessert. I *hate* cooked broccoli."

Mrs. Wright held up her hand to stop any further complaints and immediately went to phone great Aunt Opal.

Aunt Opal was a bundle of energy. She was five-foot, two inches tall and a widow. Her full name was Opal Ruby Martha Diamond Wright. Tim had once asked her why she had so many names and she said it was "on account of her parents having so many sons and only one daughter. She, being the last child, by the time she came along her parents had saved up so many girl's names that they gave all of them to her."

Great Aunt Opal was, as usual, glad to go. She was always excited to go and see new things. Though Tim thought she was a little senile sometimes, he had to admit that he did enjoy her company. She was a little near-sighted, too, and hard of hearing, but she had the most unusual optimistic way of looking at things.

"Hey Tim," Kimberly suggested. "Since Mom and Jonathan can't use their tickets, maybe we can see if Lindy and Robert can come along."

"Good idea," said Tim, "then Aunt Opal can pick on them, too."

Tim telephoned Robert. Ten minutes later, Robert called back. "Hey Tim," he said excitedly, "my mom said we can go. Washington, D.C., *here we come!*"

CHAPTER 5

Flight

"My, isn't this exciting!" said great Aunt Opal happily the next morning as their plane sped down the runway. With a deafening roar, the airplane lifted off the concrete and sailed into the clear morning sky. Aunt Opal smiled, "And you children will be glad to know that I brought your favorite dessert."

"Pumpkin pie?" asked Robert hopefully.

"No, your other favorite, *Cooked Broccoli Surprise.* Timothy, dear, why are you holding your nose? Oh, and Timothy," she said. "I noticed your shoelaces were loose. You might stumble over them, honey."

"Yes, ma'am," Tim replied, obediently leaning over to re-tie his shoes.

"My goodness, a whole wide world full of adventure," said Aunt Opal with a sparkle in her eye. "I hope we can see the pyramids at Cheops."

"But Aunt Opal, we're only going as far as Washington, D.C.," said Kimberly.

"Oh, yes, that is our plan. But you never know what might happen along the way. My, but isn't this wonderful, the five of us going to see new places."

The "seatbelts" sign went off and Aunt Opal selected a travel magazine from her bag. Putting on her glasses, she read aloud to the cousins about dream trips to the beautiful mountains of Austria, the outback of Australia, and the pyramids of Central America.

"Excuse me," interrupted a flight attendant politely from the aisle. "There's a message for the young man in the fourth seat over." The cousins looked up.

"Me?" said Robert in surprise.

"Yes," replied the attendant. "You may pick it up with the headphones–they're in the back compartment of the seat in front of you."

"Thanks," said Robert. He retrieved the white plastic headphones and slipped them on over his ears.

As Robert listened, there was a clicking sound, signaling the start of a recorded message. "Agent Kimosoggy," a man's voice began, "U.S. national security has been breached. Thank you for accepting this most vital mission."

"Right," thought Robert to himself. "Only Goofer Mike could come up with a line like that. Goofer's dad works for the airlines, so arranging something like this wouldn't be too much of a challenge."

The message continued: "Kimosoggy, as you know, the Straunsee matter is of huge international proportions. As one of America's top two secret agents, I am calling on you and Agent Toronto to find Straunsee's daughter. Furthermore, you must secure the president's briefcase and take it to the White House by 1000 hours–that's 10am Eastern Standard Time–

Friday. Every enemy agent is out to stop you. Pick up your briefcase, Portal A, Locker 9257. Beware of–."

The headphones were suddenly plucked from Robert's head. "My turn," said Tim, "What music is it?"

"It's another message from Goofer Mike," Robert replied, grabbing back the headphones and slipping them on. To Robert's dismay, the message had ended and did not repeat. "Tim, you didn't tell Goofer we were coming to Washington, D.C., did you?"

Tim was silent a moment. "Well, kind of," he admitted. "He was wanting to schedule a chess game rematch with you and I kind of told him about my famous poem recital. Why?"

"He just sent me a message calling me one of America's top two secret agents, wanting me to do some special mission for him to save America."

"What an imagination," said Tim.

"I'm afraid we're in for it now," said Robert, glancing out the window. "No telling what Goofer's dreamed up."

Outside the plane, the sky was a deep, royal blue. Looking ahead, Robert could see dark gray storm clouds gathering on the horizon. He wasn't sure why, but he had an uneasy feeling, like something important was about to happen.

When they reached their destination and the time came to leave the plane, Aunt Opal suddenly began looking around through her carry-on bags. "Oh, goodness," she said with concern. "I can't seem to find my travel mirror. Perhaps I left it in the powder room. I'd better go check."

"We'll wait for you," offered Kimberly.

"No, go ahead, dearie. I'll catch up with you at the baggage claim area."

As the Wright Cousins left the plane, Robert caught a glimpse of a large rectangular sign announcing, "PORTAL A."

"Portal A?" thought Robert. "Goofer's locker was supposed to be at that portal. I wonder if it even exists."

Spying an information booth, Robert excused himself from the girls for a moment and walked over to the booth.

"Hey, wait up," Tim called out. "Where are you going?"

"C'mon, Tim, let's go see if we can catch Goofer Mike."

"Excuse me, sir," Robert asked the man at the booth. "Are there any lockers around here?"

"Lockers? Yes sir, down that hallway on the other side of the lobby."

"Thanks," said Robert, heading toward the lockers. Robert explained to Tim about the message on the plane.

"And it said to look in locker number 9257?" asked Tim.

"Yes, and there was some kind of warning," said Robert. "But that's the part I didn't get. *Somebody* pulled the earphones off my head."

"Oh," replied Tim with a guilty grin, "the nerve of some people."

The lockers were tall, thin white ones. They began with the number 9200. At the end of the hallway, Tim and Robert spied locker 9257.

"There's really one with that number?" said Tim. "Let's see what's in it."

"Wait a minute," cautioned Robert. "If I know Goofer Mike, it's probably been booby-trapped or something. We'll have to be careful."

Robert tried the latch. It was unlocked!

The boys slowly opened the door and peeked inside. The locker contained two slim attaché cases, one stacked on top of the other. Each had a plastic nametag attached to its handle, one labeled *Kimosoggy* and the other, *Toronto*.

CHAPTER 6

Disconcerting Events

"I bet Goofer Mike has them stink-bombed or something," said Tim.

"We'll have to outsmart him," said Robert. "On the count of three, reach in and grab a briefcase and run for your life. One, two, three."

Both boys took a briefcase and raced down the hall. ***Kaboom!*** A loud explosion hurled the boys from their feet and sent them sliding down the hallway atop their attaché cases.

"Timothy Wright, you come back here," scolded Kimberly as she and Lindy watched the two boys go sliding across the lobby. "And don't run into the–." There was a double ***thunk*** as both boys hit the wall.

Kimberly went chasing after Tim. "Timothy Wright, are you hurt?" she asked when she caught up to him. Tim, covered with soot and slightly dizzy, looked up at his concerned sister. "Wow," he said, "on the scale of Robert's usual scientific explosions, I'd give this one about a five. The rollercoaster places ought to take a lesson from Robert."

"I heard that," said Robert defensively. "I do not cause explosions. Well, not on purpose, anyways. And this wasn't one of mine or one of Goofer's, either."

"What do you mean?" asked Tim. "I thought this was all Goofer Mike's doing."

"So did I," said Robert thoughtfully. "But this explosion was on the dangerous side. Maybe there's something to this Kimosoggy and Toronto stuff after all. Maybe somebody thinks we're top secret agents."

"What?" said Tim.

"I mean, maybe that recorded message on the plane—."

"And you two are supposed to be America's top two secret agents?" said Kimberly, breaking into a smile. "You, Kimosoggy, and him, Toronto?"

"It does sound kind of crazy, doesn't it," Robert replied, getting to his feet.

"Crazy isn't the word," said Kimberly. "I think that explosion knocked you silly."

"Yeah, I guess you're right," said Robert, suddenly getting a mischievous grin on his face. "But wouldn't it be fun to *act* like secret agents? Tim, let's hang onto these briefcases for a while. They're pretty cool. I mean, they even have *TOP SECRET* stenciled across the sides of them."

Robert cleared his throat and said in an official voice, "Agent Toronto, since we have been provided with the latest in *TOP SECRET* attachés, I propose we use them. Note the custom, locking wrist strap; place it around your left wrist so your writing hand is free."

"Timothy, don't you dare," said Kimberly.

"Right-o," said Tim, enjoying the annoyed look on his sister's face. Tim locked on the security strap and asked, "What next, Agent Kimosoggy?"

"We must synchronize our watches," said Robert.

"Hey, you *nuts*," said Kimberly with an embarrassed smile. "People are beginning to look at us."

"Watches, synchronize them," Robert continued. "Upon my word. 3-2-1. Mark."

"Synchronized," said Tim.

The onlooking crowd was growing larger by the second. "Those two boys over there," the cousins heard someone say.

"Robert, this is not the time for acting," warned Lindy. "Cut it out or airport security is going to haul us away."

Robert glanced mechanically from side to side. "Yes," he whispered in a secret agent manner, "I see what you mean. Meet at the luggage carousel. Emergency plan DS."

"Which one is that?" Kimberly whispered to Lindy.

"Distract and Scram," Lindy replied. "Robert will distract and we'll scram."

"Ah-HUM, excuse me, folks," said Robert, holding his hand up in the air like a policeman directing traffic. "Excuse me, may I please have your attention? Everything is all right. My partner, here–Agent Morgleborgleburger–and I–," he nodded toward Tim, "have everything under control."

"That's right," said Tim, smiling and nodding at the crowd. "We do. It's all under control–everything is–we've got it."

Kimberly and Lindy were quickly fading into the crowd.

"Yes, so here's what we need you to do," Robert continued, now motioning toward the man in the information booth. "That is Mr. Kalinski-Smyrdi-bairdy of the *official* airport information booth staff. He will be happy to answer *all* of your questions."

The crowd immediately pushed toward the surprised

airport employee and began bombarding him with questions. Taking advantage of the confusion they had created, Robert and Tim crouched down and slipped through the pressing onlookers. Once to the outer edge of the crowd, they ran off to meet the girls.

When the boys reached the luggage area, they spied Kimberly and Lindy. “We can’t find Aunt Opal,” Kimberly announced.

“What?” said Tim, glancing down at his shoelaces apprehensively.

“I’ve reviewed our departure off the plane,” said Lindy. “I don’t think she got off.”

“But Tim’s supposed to be at his poetry recital in forty-five minutes,” said Robert. “What are we going to do?”

“We’d better find a taxi,” said Kimberly.

“Right,” said Lindy. “Aunt Opal knows our itinerary and she’ll know we headed there.”

“There’s only one problem,” said Robert. “Do you guys have any money for the taxi?”

“That’s right,” said Kimberly. “Aunt Opal has all the money.”

Everyone quickly dug through their pockets. Adding all their funds together, the four cousins had a grand total of $37.

“I hope that’s enough to get us there. Otherwise, we’re going to have to do a lot of walking,” said Kimberly.

“I just remembered,” said Tim. “We don’t have to worry about money. Once we get to the recital, the PoemNet people will give us our money for the vacation.”

“That’s right,” said Robert as they headed out to hail a taxi. “Let’s go.”

The cousins made it to the large concert hall with less than five minutes to spare. Leaping out of their taxi, they quickly paid the driver and raced up the long stairway toward the front of the building.

At the top of the stairs, they discovered a wide drive with drop off zones. "Hey," said Tim huffing and puffing. "Why didn't that taxi guy let us off up here?"

Glancing in both directions to make sure no cars were coming, the cousins dashed across the street and up to the large glass doors at the main entry. Pushing on the thick doors, they found them locked. The cousins hurriedly tried the other doors; they, too, were locked. With noses to the glass, the cousins peered into the luxurious but darkened lobby.

"Why aren't the lights on?" asked Tim. "Where is everybody?"

Lindy found an announcement taped to a ticket booth window nearby. The message read:

> **"We are sorry for the inconvenience, but the Poetry Reading of "Knight and Day" by Master Timothy Wright, Esquire, Poet-at-large, has been postponed because of today's airport bomb blast. To ensure appropriate security, we have rescheduled him for tomorrow night at the request of the President of the United States of America."**

"The author is always the last to know," lamented Tim, shaking his head from side-to-side. "Doesn't anybody believe in calling anymore?"

"Did Tim say what I think he said?" said Kimberly.

"Well," said Tim, a little uncomfortably. "People need to be more *responsible* sometimes—."

"Timothy Wright?" said Kimberly with surprise. "Are you feeling okay?"

Lindy suddenly grasped her brother's arm. "Robert," she said, "we forgot our luggage in the taxi!"

Panic-stricken, the four cousins raced back across the street and scanned the roadway below. Their taxi was nowhere to be seen!

CHAPTER 7

Vanilla Shakes and Onion Rings

"Bummersville," said Robert. "That taxi guy got away with everything."

"You don't think he did it on purpose, do you?" asked Lindy.

"Of course," said Tim. "Anybody that would make us run up all those steps instead of dropping us off up here, *has* to be a crook."

Not knowing what else to do, the cousins decided to sit down and wait for Aunt Opal to arrive. They waited and waited and waited. As the sun sunk lower in the sky, a cold breeze began to chill them. The cousins turned up their collars and zipped their coats to keep warm. Car after car sped by on the street below, but still no Aunt Opal. Worry was beginning to gnaw away at their confidence in their aunt.

At long last, the cousins heard a car climbing the hill. It was a yellow taxi!

"Finally," said Tim, leaping eagerly to his feet. The taxi slowed in front of the building, but spying the four cousins, the driver stepped on the accelerator and sped away.

"Did you guys get a look at the driver?" asked Kimberly.

"Yes," said Lindy. "It wasn't Aunt Opal *or* our driver."

"There's only one explanation for this," said Tim. "Aunt Opal doesn't like us anymore. She's abandoned us."

"Not Aunt Opal," said Robert, watching the taxi disappear in the distance. "She probably just got lost. Otherwise, she would have left us with the *Cooked Broccoli Surprise*. Lindy, how much money do we have? I'm getting hungry."

Lindy thought for a second. "Subtracting the price of our taxi ride," she said. "We should now have exactly one dollar and twenty-five cents."

"Bummer," said Robert dejectedly. "Not even enough for a vanilla shake and onion rings."

"Maybe we've got some power bars in our attachés," said Tim.

"No good," said Robert. "I tried to get mine open in the taxi, but it's locked shut."

As the cousins returned to watching the road below, Robert absent-mindedly fiddled with his wristwatch. Glancing down, he suddenly remembered an experiment he'd been working on before they had left home. "Hey, guys," Robert announced excitedly. "I know what we can do."

With the cousins looking curiously on, Robert twisted the dial on his watch, raising up a miniature antenna. Using a pen and a small magnifying glass, he punched in several numbers.

"What are you doing?" asked Tim.

"Looking for Aunt Opal," Robert said matter-of-factly.

"In your watch?" said Tim.

"Course not," said Robert, still concentrating on his watch. "Search," he said aloud to his watch. The screen stayed the same. "Search," said Robert. "Rats, the voice recognition isn't working right now." He typed in the word "search" and watched in satisfaction as the tiny screen displayed the word "Search." "I'm just trying to reach my computer back home and through that get to the airline files," he explained.

"Don't you have to be hooked up to a phone line or something?" asked Kimberly.

"Not anymore," said Robert. "I made a satellite link."

"With your watch?" asked Kimberly incredulously.

"Hush, Kimberly," said Lindy. "Let him work."

Robert typed in more commands, followed by Aunt Opal's name. "Great," he remarked aloud. "The airport computer wants Aunt Opal's full name before it will give me an answer. How am I supposed to remember all her names?"

"You mean you got through?" said Kimberly in amazement.

"Of course he did," Lindy said proudly. "Robert can do anything. He's my brother."

"Anything except remember Aunt Opal's name," said Robert.

"That's what sisters are for," said Lindy. "Great Aunt Opal's full name is Opal Ruby Martha Diamond Wright."

"Are you sure?" said Tim.

"With her photographic memory, Lindy never forgets a name—or an encyclopedia," said Robert as he typed in the information. "Thanks, Sis," he said, and pressed *ENTER*.

Hearing two beeps, the cousins huddled closely around Robert's watch. "What's it say?" asked Kimberly.

"Aunt Opal," Robert announced, glancing through the watch's small magnifying lens, "is at this time somewhere out over the Atlantic Ocean. She's at about 25,000 feet altitude and she's due to land in London, England, in about 7 hours."

"Oh no," replied Kimberly, shaking her head at their aunt's predicament. "What do we do now?"

"Can't you call the plane back or something?" asked Tim.

"Not yet," Robert replied. "I haven't developed that technology."

In the tense silence that followed, a smile gradually crept into the corners of Lindy's mouth. "Aunt Opal always *did* want to see London," she said matter-of-factly.

"Poor Aunt Opal," said Kimberly, breaking into a grin. "She *does* have a time of it. I bet she got stuck in the powder room."

"The thing I'm worried about is her flight," said Robert, looking up from his watch. "The computer says it's a round-the-world flight. If she doesn't get off in England—."

"Wow," remarked Tim, glancing down uneasily at his shoelaces again. "I hope she brings me back a boomerang from Australia."

"Timothy Wright," said Kimberly. "I hope she does no such thing. Why, I hope she gets right off that plane in England; boomerangs are much too dangerous."

Having solved the mysterious disappearance of their great aunt, the four cousins set about to solve their current crisis, that of *no* money, *no* luggage, *no* food, and *no* place to stay.

If you've ever been in their shoes, it's a very scary feeling, especially in a large city. Totally unfamiliar with the city they were in, they began retracing the route the taxi had taken them, and thanks to Lindy's photographic memory, they knew exactly the way to go. As they walked, they tried to think of what to do next.

The cousins' trek led them through a city park. The streetlights were just flickering on and people were going home. Home to their nice, warm, secure homes.

"Let's find a police station," said Kimberly. "We could find help—."

"Tim," interrupted Robert. "Do you remember what that computer message said back home—the one about our Delta Star flight?" Tim shook his head "no."

"You mean the one about Kimosoggy and Toronto?" asked Lindy.

Robert looked at his twin sister. "Yeah, the one I thought Goofer Mike sent us."

"The one that started out 'Top Priority—Alpha Command, Memorize and Destroy?'" continued Lindy.

"Yes," replied Robert. "If I could only just remember what it said. Hey, wait a minute, Lindy, how did you know about it?"

"It was on your desk when I went in to borrow your stapler," Lindy said. "But don't worry, I returned it."

"Lindy, you can have my stapler," said Robert excitedly. "What else did the note say?"

Lindy closed her eyes, searching her photographic memory. "Let's see. I walked in—boy your desk was messy—little bits of potato chips all over," she said, opening her eyes again.

"The note, the note," urged Robert. "What did the note say?"

"Oh yeah." Lindy said, closing her eyes again. "The note. I can see it now, it says, 'From Robert. 'My Dearest Susan—.'"

"Susan?" interrupted Tim. "Robert, I thought you liked Elizabeth."

"I do—I mean—aw."

"All right," Lindy laughed, "it said: **Top Priority—Alpha Command. Memorize and destroy. Locate Katrina Straunsee, Attaché—at all costs.**"

"Quick, somebody give me a pen?" said Robert. "I want to write it down, so we'll have it."

Tim retrieved a pen from his front pocket and handed it to Robert. Kimberly had a small piece of paper.

"Okay," said Robert, "go ahead, Lindy."

"DELTA STAR 246-RES: SMITH & JONES. DEST: PORT A, LOCK 9257. Next line. **WES-SAV**," Lindy began. "**1073–**."

"Wait a second," said Robert. "Slow down."

"WES-SAV 107345000-3291 UNCLOSED ON INQUIRY. That's it."

Tim looked at what Robert had written down. "What kind of message is that?"

CHAPTER 8

ATM Attack

To Robert's surprise, the message was beginning to make sense. "Hey guys, take a look at this," he said, studying the information Lindy had given him. "Delta Star 246. That's the airplane flight that got us here. Lock 9257, that's the locker where we found these indestructible attaché cases. Each part of the message has come to mean something so far. So maybe this WES-SAV stands for—."

Robert glanced around, grasping for some way to make sense of it all. "Maybe WES-SAV is the people that are going to pay for our stay out here."

"The PoemNet people?" asked Tim, wrinkling his nose at the idea. "Hey, maybe they were actually trying to get the message to me?"

"Don't be silly," said Kimberly. "They got ahold of you on the Internet, didn't they?"

"Yeah, but I was over at Robert's house that day, remember?" said Tim. "Maybe they have some kind of magnetic Internet thing that tracks you around like a dog. Besides, who else would be wanting to give us money?"

Kimberly shrugged her shoulders.

"Forget who," said Lindy. "Let's just focus on *how.* Maybe WES-SAV stands for WESTERN SAVINGS. And the numbers are an account number they've opened up for our expenses!"

"Sounds good to me," said Robert. "Let's try it."

After a quick search, the cousins located a WESTERN SAVINGS branch in a small, nearby mall. Racing up to the front door, they found it locked.

"Must be after hours," said Kimberly, as they all peered inside.

"The whole place looks empty," said Tim.

"Maybe they have an ATM around here," Lindy suggested.

Stepping back, the cousins spied an ATM two stores away.

"All in favor of not sleeping on the sidewalk tonight, say 'aye'," Robert said, breaking into a run. Arriving at the ATM, the cousins noted a *Western Savings* logo across the top of it.

"Just one problem," said Kimberly with disappointment, "it takes a card."

"Don't look at me," said Tim, "For some reason, Mom doesn't trust me with her debit card. I only wanted to buy a new car."

Robert glanced down at the attaché case still attached to his wrist. The plastic Kimosoggy nametag caught his eye. On a hunch, he slipped the tag off the handle and held it up to the ATM slot. "Maybe this will work," he said, pushing it into the slot.

The ATM "clicked" and, somewhere deep inside the machine, a motor whirred into action. To Robert's right, a small door slid open, revealing rows of lighted buttons with numbers on them.

"Cool," said Tim, eager to push a button. "Let's get some money and find a smorgasbord, I'm starving."

"Wait a minute, Tim," said Robert. "Let's figure out how much money we're going to need for tonight. We don't want to use it all up at once."

"We'll need about $200 for two rooms," Lindy suggested.

"And dinner," Tim said hungrily. "Don't forget that—and breakfast and lunch."

"And a little extra," added Kimberly.

"Okay, how about 285 dollars?" Robert said with a smile.

"Better add fifty cents," said Tim. "In case we have to leave a tip."

"$285.50 it is," said Robert cheerfully as he punched in the amount. When he hit the enter key, the machine buzzed, denoting an error had been made. Robert typed in the number again, and again it buzzed.

"Maybe you have to round it to the nearest dollar," said Lindy. "Make it 290, even."

Robert typed in $290. The machine displayed the number 290 and the word "Acknowledge."

"Punch *yes*," Tim said excitedly.

Robert did, and a small hatch opened, revealing a thick stack of money. "Thank goodness," said Robert with a big smile on his face as he reached in and took the money. "Now let's go get something to eat."

"What a cheap machine," said Kimberly, glancing at the cash in Robert's hand. "It just gave us a bunch of one-dollar bills. They usually do twenties."

"Who cares," said Tim. "As long as it's enough to get us some food and a place to stay."

Robert gave the money to Lindy to count. As Lindy started thumbing through the money, her face paled. The more she counted, the paler she became.

"Robert," Lindy said, "this isn't $290."

"No?" Robert replied, his moment of triumph suddenly dashed.

Lindy squared up the stack of bills and handed them back to Robert. "No, it's a little bit more. These aren't one-dollar bills; they're *thousands.* Robert, this machine just gave us 290 *thousand* dollars!"

Robert looked at the money. His eyes grew big with shock. He tried to give the money back to Lindy; Lindy wouldn't take it. He tried to hand it to Kimberly, but she wouldn't take it, either. He started to hand it to Tim. No, that was too much money for Tim.

Fearing some big mistake, Robert turned to the ATM machine and tried stuffing some of the money back into it. It wouldn't take it, either. Suddenly, an ear-piercing siren started blaring and the access door on the ATM slammed shut.

"Somebody's robbing that ATM over there," an onlooker shouted. People poured out of the stores to see what was going on.

Among the crowd that had gathered several stores away, Robert saw members of a youth gang. Spying the thick wad of money in Robert's hand, the gang members started heading over to get in on the action.

"They've got baseball bats," Kimberly said with concern.

"And there's at least fifteen of them," said Lindy, gripping Robert's arm. "What should we do?"

"Kimberly, you and Tim cover for Lindy," said Robert as he secretly slipped the money into Lindy's hands. "Take three steps backwards—away from the gang—and then *run for it.*"

Taking the cash, Lindy quickly shoved it into the front pocket of her jeans and nervously stepped away. Tim and Kimberly followed her.

Robert remained at the ATM, pretending to punch buttons to keep the gang's attention.

"One, two," Robert counted silently. "Three." Backing away, he turned and ran for his life!

Caught off guard, the gang of roughnecks started after him. They were fast runners—used to the bad life on the street—and fanned out to trap Robert. Turning a corner with the gang in full pursuit, Robert saw the other cousins ahead. "Run for it!" he shouted, pounding after them.

Turning another corner, the cousins spotted a fire station. Two trucks with sirens blaring were just pulling out onto the street, heading away from the cousins.

Robert glanced back. The gang was gaining on him! Looking ahead, he saw Lindy and the others starting to falter. Tim was slowed by his attaché case just as Robert was. "The truck," Robert shouted to them. "Get on the fire truck!"

Seeing it as their last chance to escape, the three cousins caught up with the rearmost truck and jumped aboard. Still clinging onto his attaché case, Robert felt his legs turning to lead as he raced after them.

"Robert, come on," Lindy called out from the rear platform of the truck. With one hand on the truck's rear railing, Lindy reached out for her brother. "Robert. Grab my hand!"

Lindy screamed in horror as Robert stumbled as he left the sidewalk. "Robert, they're right behind you!"

Robert lunged forward, touching Lindy's fingers, and then lost them again. The fire truck was gaining speed.

"You can do it," called out Lindy.

Summoning all the energy he had left, Robert leapt toward his sister's outstretched arm and caught her wrist. The weight nearly pulled Lindy off the truck, but Kimberly grabbed his wrist, too, and they both pulled him aboard.

Closing in for the kill, the gang leader dove for Robert's attaché case—missing it by inches—and slammed into the pavement.

Lindy clung to her twin brother as they sped away on the back of the truck. "Oh Robert," she said, sobbing with relief. "I was so afraid you weren't going to make it."

"Me too," Robert gasped, trying to catch his breath. "Me too."

CHAPTER 9

Race for America

It was to be a routine mission. Colonel Steve Green, a U.S. Air Force test pilot, was going to make a final test run across the Atlantic Ocean from a secret base in the United Kingdom. He would be flying at night. If all went well, the plane he was piloting, the top secret YF121-LC (YF standing for *prototype fighter*), would be advanced to operational status and become America's latest supersonic stealth fighter. Though the plane was a two-seater, he would be flying it alone, or so he thought.

At "go" hour, Colonel Steve Green slipped into his flight suit and helmet and strapped himself in. He ran through the check-off list and taxied out of the secret hangar. A light rain pattered on the plane's canopy, bringing visibility down to zero. That didn't matter, though, because he had the latest night-vision equipment. Colonel Green turned the plane onto the runway. The YF121 had VTOL–Vertical Takeoff or Landing capabilities–but he wasn't using them tonight. He was saving his fuel for the flight to America.

"Eagle 1, cleared for takeoff," announced the tower. Colonel Green increased the thrust of his engines and released the brakes. The YF121 sped down the runway and leapt into the dark sky. The glow of two bright tongues of exhaust fire was all that could be seen of the midnight black plane.

"Clear," cheerfully radioed 25-year-old Colonel Green.

"Roger. Enjoy," called back the tower.

"Roger wilco." Colonel Green glanced at his watch. He was timing the flight, hoping to set a new personal record. He made a wide banking turn as he gained altitude and pointed the plane's nose toward the North American continent. "U.S.A., here we come," he said gleefully.

The plane rose swiftly, leaving soggy England behind. "I haven't had a good American hamburger in a month," said Colonel Green with anticipation.

Breaking out of the clouds, Colonel Green's plane entered a whole new world. The moon was a beautiful white ball far to the west. Below it, Colonel Green beheld the vast Atlantic Ocean stretching out as far as his eyes could see. He felt like he was among the stars in heaven.

Fifteen minutes out, Colonel Green rendezvoused with a tanker plane and topped off his fuel tanks. Shortly after leaving the tanker, Colonel Green felt a tap on his shoulder and nearly jumped out of the plane.

"Who's there?" Colonel Green called out, trying to catch a glimpse of the seat behind him. It appeared to be empty. He felt the tap again. "Who is it?" Colonel Green asked.

This time Colonel Green thought he heard a faint female voice and glanced nervously at his altimeter. "Who could be hitchhiking at this altitude?" he wondered. The thought of angels did cross his mind for a second but he dismissed it. "Who's there?" he called out again.

"Me," replied a shaky voice.

"Me who?" asked Colonel Green. "And don't say Darth Vader or I'll punch out your ejection seat!"

"I am a friend...of Yoda," came a fearful young woman's reply.

"Yoda?" said Colonel Green. "Yoda? That's a name I haven't heard since...*Princess Katrina of Gütenberg?!*"

"Please don't be upset, Mr. Green, sir," said Princess Katrina, her normally sweet and pleasant voice still trembling.

Amazingly, there was no foreign accent in Katrina's voice. Her mother, Lady Sutherlee, had come from England. Katrina and her three sisters had watched many American classic movies while growing up. Katrina was good at languages and had mastered, among several others, American English.

"I'm not upset," Colonel Green replied. "You just kind of scared me to death, that's all."

"Please don't make me go back to England, Mr. Green," said the sixteen-year-old princess. "I need your help."

"How on earth—what are you doing here?" Colonel Green replied. "And how did you get past base security?"

"The men who kidnapped me—they put me in here. They were going to steal this plane, but you got to it before they were ready. I heard them talking about putting something in the bottom of your plane."

"Did you see what it was?" asked Colonel Green.

"It was some kind of metal tank or barrel."

"Did they put it in the bomb bay?"

"Yes, I believe so," replied Katrina, her voice growing stronger. "I heard them say they wanted to drop it somewhere over a city in America."

"Princess, I'm not sure, but you may have just saved Washington, D.C.!" said Colonel Green.

Six bright blips suddenly appeared on the YF121's radar screen. Colonel Green eyed them. None of the blips had IFF—*Identification Friend or Foe*—which meant he had to assume the worst: the blips represented enemy planes. The planes were coming in from three different directions: two from the right, two from the left, and two from the rear. All were traveling at very high speeds. Colonel Green nudged his plane to the right. The enemy planes mimicked him. He veered to the left. They followed him again. "That's weird," he thought, "they're not supposed to be able to see us. We're in a stealth plane."

"What's wrong?" asked Katrina, sensing Colonel Green's change of manner.

"We've got six planes on our tail."

"Can they catch us?" asked Katrina.

"Not if I can help it," said Colonel Green, throttling up the plane's engines. Colonel Green knew he could outrun the planes to the rear, but it was the four vectoring in from the sides that bothered him. He trimmed the plane, watching his instruments closely.

A loud warning buzzer suddenly sounded. Glancing at his radar, Colonel Green saw that several of the planes were gaining on him. They were now nearing firing range and were "locking on" their targeting radars. The new YF121 and its occupants had just been "painted."

Colonel Green kicked on the afterburners. They flared bright orange and the YF121 leapt forward. The enemy threat buzzer stopped. "We're losing them, Princess," said Colonel Green.

Another group of blips suddenly appeared on the radar. Four more planes to the front left. The new enemy planes had just locked-on and were preparing to launch missiles.

"Are you strapped in, Princess?" asked Colonel Green.

"Yes. Why?"

"We're in deep trouble. These guys want to play *chicken.*"

CHAPTER 10

The Game

After riding their fire truck to its fiery destination, the Wright cousins got an appropriate lecture from the firefighters in the cab about how dangerous their act of "hitching" a ride had been.

The cousins soon found lodging in a very fancy hotel named *The Golden Chariot.* At first, they got some flak about trying to pay with one of their $1000 bills, but the hotel manager finally relented and had given them a suite with separate rooms for the girls and boys. Starved, the cousins had eaten three courses of "chicken nuggets under glass" and polished off two complete cherry pies with vanilla ice cream.

During their dinner, Robert and Tim had discovered a latch mechanism and had gotten the attaché straps off their wrists.

When dinner was over, the cousins settled into their respective rooms, Kimberly and Lindy in one and Tim and Robert in the other. Kimberly and Lindy each phoned their moms with the news of the day.

Robert and Tim, meanwhile, were trying to figure out how to open their attaché cases. The cases were sturdily built of stainless steel. Tim finally gave up and switched on the TV. He located a cartoon channel and was soon locked in.

"Hey Tim," Robert called out. "I think I found something. There's a sliding panel on the top edge of the case. Looks like the ATM card might fit in it." Retrieving his plastic card, Robert slid it into the slot and waited. The attaché unlocked!

"What's in it?" asked Tim, still watching his cartoons.

Robert released the case's two latches and carefully opened it. Inside were a sand-colored trench coat, secret agent hat, several button radios, and a hand-sized computer. "Looks like everything a secret agent needs except Broccoli Bombs," Robert called out.

Tim grinned about the Broccoli Bombs. Robert had accidentally invented them in chemistry class one day. He had been trying to invent a new food to solve world hunger. The secret ingredients of *The Bomb,* as Robert and Tim called it, were known only to themselves.

"Wow," Tim said, turning away from the TV, "that's cool. I wonder if I have that kind of stuff in mine?"

Following Robert's lead, Tim carefully opened his attaché and found identical items inside.

Robert searched the pockets of the trench coat. He found a pair of sunglasses and put them on. "Hey Tim, what do you think of my new shades?"

"Cool," replied Tim. "Let me see them."

"Wait a second," said Robert, his eyes fixed on the television screen. "Tim, these glasses change the picture."

"Let's see," said Tim.

"Check your case. Maybe you've got a pair, too."

Tim found an identical pair of glasses in his trench coat and slipped them on. "Wow," he said. "It's like a video game. I wonder how we play." Opening the small hand-held computer from his case, Tim switched it on and started pushing buttons. To his great pleasure, he found the buttons changed the images on his glasses. "Hey, this is neat," he said. "I don't even need to look at the television with mine. These glasses are their own screen."

"You're right," said Robert, curiously.

"Try this button," said Tim. "It brings up some cool pictures of the earth." Robert did and soon they were both enjoying the amazing game.

Accidentally clicking a button twice, Tim brought up an interesting airplane game. "Hey Robert, tap the blue button twice."

The new game's scenario was that of a single plane being chased by a large number of enemy planes. "How do you think we play this one?" Tim asked.

"I don't know," said Robert. "But I can guess which plane we get to be."

"The lone one," replied Tim, nodding his head. "Do you think we can do it?"

Robert, always one to love figuring out how things work, set out to find the answer. First, he tried the different buttons on the computer. None seemed to allow them to interact with the game.

"Hurry Robert," said Tim, watching the airplanes in his glasses. "The bad guys are gaining on us, our plane."

Not finding anything in the attaché case that seemed to work, Robert fell back on his next line of defense, his wristwatch. Pushing the power button on his band, a small sentence of red words appeared and blinked on his sunglasses. "Wow, did you see that?" asked Robert.

"Did you do that?" asked Tim.

"Yeah, I'll try something else," said Robert.

"Okay," said Tim, "but you'd better hurry. Our plane is just about to get creamed!"

Glancing down at his watch, Robert quickly asked for the game scenario. Hitting the enter key, red words began scrolling across his glasses: "A lone YF121 is being chased by four Mark Fives and two Mark Fours. To the left front of the YF121 are four Mark Sixes. Request direction."

"Hey," said Tim. "That looks like the plane you and Jonathan flew in the desert while we were looking for that lost Spanish treasure ship."

"Sure does," said Robert, typing in the words "YF121 status?" Again, the red words appeared: "Operating at governor-set speed of one-half throttle. Engines okay. Weapons okay. Life support okay. Armament: twelve heat-seeker decoys; chaff; two high-energy laser cannons."

"C'mon Robert, do something," said Tim. "The bad guys are locked-on and getting ready to launch their missiles!"

"Okay, okay," said Robert, don't rush me. "Um, let's see," he said, typing in some commands on his wristwatch. "Override governor. Move power to full throttle."

"Robert, they're launching at us!"

"All right, just hang on," said Robert. "Launch decoys. Status?"

"Enemy planes launching three missiles. Red alert. Near miss!"

* * *

Several thousand miles away, Colonel Green and the princess felt their plane shudder as a missile burst close behind them. Their decoy had worked, but it was close. Pushing for more power against the plane's governor, Colonel Green felt the controls suddenly move. The words he'd been praying for appeared on his heads-up display: RAMJETS ENABLED.

"Princess Katrina," Colonel Green said excitedly. "Hold on tight. We're about to make MACH–."

The ramjets kicked on and the plane shot forward like a rocket!

* * *

"Robert," said Tim. "You did it. We're losing the planes in back. But what about the planes in front?"

"Right," said Robert anxiously typing away on his watch. "Frontal assault threat?"

"Four Mark Sixes. Missiles armed and launching."

"Oh wow," said Robert. "Let's see. We can't outrun the heat-seeking missiles. Um. We need more firepower. What have we got in the way of surface ships? Nothing."

"What about submarines?" asked Tim.

Robert typed in "submarines?"

"Submarines: 3 Western Atlantic, 4 Eastern Atlantic. Capability: Torpedoes and Cruise Missiles."

"Cruise missiles?" said Tim. "Aren't those the big things they blow up bunkers and stuff with?"

"I think so," said Robert. "That won't work. Oh boy, what can we do? Let's try—."

Robert typed in "Access Mark Six Aircraft: Deactivate weapons. Reduce speed to one-fifth."

* * *

On the verge of victory, the Mark Six pilots suddenly found their planes slowing to a snail's pace, some even threatening to fall from the sky.

"Squadron Leader," radioed one of the pilots. "I am losing speed—I think my engine is burning out—and my rockets won't launch."

"Me also," called in another. "And my throttle, she is not working."

The Squadron Leader didn't answer. He was having problems of his own. Having been on the verge of ultimate triumph, he was now beginning to have fears about being sent to a slave labor camp instead.

"Get your planes going," the leader commanded his pilots. "We cannot fail. Launch all rockets!"

Eyeing the weird happenings via his radar, Colonel Green was just as puzzled about his opponent's maneuvers as they were. But Colonel Green was having problems of his own. He couldn't get his throttle to back off and his plane was now approaching Mach 6, almost 4,400 miles per hour. The leading edges of the plane's wings were glowing red-hot; the plane was getting too hot to touch!

* * *

"That's showing them," said Tim. "What about all those guys behind our plane?"

"Okay," said Robert, feeling a little less cramped. "Let's try reversing their engine thrusters."

"Can we do that?" asked Tim.

"I don't know," replied Robert. "We can try."

"Maybe we ought to give them a little warning before we do," said Tim.

"Good idea," said Robert, typing away. "Attention Crews, Marks 4, 5, and 6: Due to unforeseen circumstances, your planes are about to go into reverse. This will not be good for your transmissions—."

"Planes don't have transmissions, do they?" asked Tim.

"Course not," said Robert, "It's just a figure of speech."

Robert finished his message to the enemy planes: "I recommend you pull your ejection seat handle or you might not survive. Sincerely, Kimosoggy and Toronto. Ten-four, over and out. And may the force *not* be with you."

"Good," said Tim, "I like the part about the ejection seats. It makes it sound official."

Robert and Tim watched gleefully as plane after plane's pilot ejected. "Looks like we've got two stubborn guys," said Tim. "Guess we'd better teach them a lesson."

"Right," said Robert, typing in "seat eject" commands for the two planes. He pushed "enter" and ***kaboom***, there they went, flying out of their planes at a hundred miles an hour.

"We did it," said Tim, smiling at the fact that their plane was the only one left in the sky. "Boy, you've got a great watch. When are you going to build one for me?"

Robert grinned. "Timbo," he said cheerfully, "what do you say we pick up all those poor soggy bad guys and put them in jail?"

"How?" asked Tim. "Shouldn't we just let the sharks get them?"

"Now Tim, they've been good enough to ditch all their planes in the ocean for us, the least we can do is arrange a little rescue and a nice warm cell."

"I guess so," Tim replied reluctantly. "But what if they escape and come back in the next level of the game?"

But Robert wasn't listening; he was already typing in a whole string of commands.

*　　　*　　　*

Far out in the cold Atlantic Ocean, the enemy pilots were bobbing up and down in the water. At least their life jackets worked! To the downed-pilots' horror, a large fin appeared in the water. Rising from the cold, black ocean, the fin grew bigger.

"It is a sea monster," shouted one of the men.

"No, it is the Bermuda Triangle," shouted another.

"It is a UFO," wailed another. "I told you we should not have attacked that American plane!"

High atop the fin, a blindingly bright light appeared, probing the night sea around it. "Hands up, everybody," directed a navy officer's voice over a megaphone. "You are now the prisoners of the U.S.S. Swordnop. Please drop your weapons and prepare to board. I don't exactly know who you all are, but you have *Kimosoggy* and *Toronto* to thank for your rescue."

*　　　　*　　　　*

Having ordered out his submarines and surface vessels, Robert next turned his attention to the condition of their victorious YF121 airplane. "YF121 status check: Speed–sustainable. Weapons–armed. Crew–tired but happy. Fuel–WARNING: DANGEROUSLY LOW."

"Robert," said Tim. "We'd better find a gas station. And make it *full serve* because I don't do windshields."

"Right," said Robert, scanning the area around the YF121. "I don't see any bases where we can land, maybe we can find an air tanker to refuel us. Let's see–air tankers. There's a tanker in the air right now over–I think that's Oklahoma. No, that's too far away. Wait, here's one off the coast of Massachusetts, let's try that one." Robert clicked on it. "Bummer," he said. "It seems to be refueling an SR93."

"Well, tell him to break it off," said Tim. "This is an emergency!"

"Sounds good," said Robert, beginning to type in a command. "Boy, remind me to fix the voice command feature in my watch; this typing is getting to be the pits."

As Robert neared the end of his command line, the red words on his glass' lenses began blinking on and off.

"Hey, what's going on?" said Tim.

"We're in trouble," Robert replied, hurrying to complete the line. "BREAK OFF AND FUEL YF121 IMMEDIATELY." But just as Robert hit the "enter" key, the words disappeared from the screen.

"Hey, where'd the words go?" asked Tim.

"Nowhere," replied Robert with a distressed look on his face. "My watch batteries just went dead."

Tim and Robert watched as the lone plane continued its course to America.

"Bummer," Tim said. "We beat Level 1 and we can't even save the game. We're going to have to do it all over again."

Out over the Atlantic, Colonel Green was having troubles of his own. His plane was stuck on full throttle and it was burning up all his fuel. He needed to find a tanker and find it *fast!*

CHAPTER 11

America

"Eagle Command, this is Eagle 1," radioed Colonel Green. "Am low on fuel. Request tanker."

"Copy, Eagle 1. We'll see what we can do for you."

"Roger," Colonel Green replied, finally getting his throttle to free up. His Heads-up Display suddenly showed an unidentified plane—a bogey—far ahead of him at very low altitude. Whoever it was, they were trying to avoid radar by flying "on the deck."

"Eagle 1, this is Eagle Command. We're picking up a lone plane ahead of you."

"Roger," said Colonel Green. "I just saw it, too. Any idea what it is?"

"Negative. We've lost it again. Suggest you take evasive action."

"No can do," Colonel Green said grimly. "I'm too low on fuel."

"Just a minute. We've just received information that it may be an Air Force Tanker that's been missing, but it's way off course. Continue defensive stature until we verify."

"Copy. Please hurry, Eagle Command." Colonel Green glanced at his low fuel warning light.

"Affirmative, Eagle 1," Eagle Command finally broke in. "It is an air tanker. Will transfer tanker's message to your frequency and scramble."

"Read you loud and clear," Colonel Green replied happily. "Go ahead."

"This is Golf Eagle Oscar," said the tanker pilot. "Acknowledge."

"Copy, Golf Eagle Oscar. This is Eagle 1. Am in need of fuel."

"I'll have to clear it through–."

"Oh, dearie me," interrupted a new voice. "Young man, this is no time to involve a bunch of middlemen in a bureaucracy. We have lots of fuel and that nice young man evidently needs some. Didn't your mother teach you about sharing and keeping your shoes tied and such?"

"No, it couldn't be," said Colonel Green, recognizing the new voice. "Great Aunt Opal, is that you?"

"Nephew Steve?" Aunt Opal radioed back. "Martha's daughter's son's brother? What are you doing out here at this late hour of the night?"

"Auntie, what are you doing in an Air Force tanker?"

"While on my way to Washington, D.C., with Kevin and Rebecca and Kurt and Connie's kids, I accidentally ran into General Thomas in England. He lined me up with this wonderful flight back to America to meet them. I'm their chaperone, you know."

"Oh," said Colonel Green. "Well, please tell your pilot that if he gives me some fuel that it will lighten his plane. Then you'll be able to get to Washington, D.C., faster."

"Okay, okay," said the tanker pilot, eager to get on with his flight. "If you two will promise to postpone your conversation until later, I'll be more than happy to fill you up."

The tanker gained altitude. A crew member on the tanker plane lowered the plane's long refueling boom pipe and gave Colonel Green clearance to approach.

Flipping a switch, Colonel Green opened the fuel hatch on the top of his plane's fuselage and vectored his plane into position. Soon Colonel Green's plane was taking on fuel.

"Full," the boom man said a short time later. "You're clear to go."

"Thanks," said Colonel Green, slowing his plane to break away. Once clear of the tanker plane, Colonel Green cheerfully throttled up his engines and set his course for America. "Princess Katrina," he said over the intercom. "There's absolutely nothing like a full load of fuel to cheer up your day."

The remainder of the flight to America went like clockwork. Using his Alpha Priority, Colonel Green arranged for a base to land at and transportation to Washington, D.C. They were to meet with the President of the United States in the early hours of the morning.

Security was tight as Colonel Green touched the YF121 down at an airbase in Virginia. Regular personnel had been given leave and cleared from the base. Alpha and other Special Forces troops had been brought in to protect the area. No unauthorized personnel would be allowed within one mile of the base perimeter. Upon instructions, Colonel Green taxied the plane into an awaiting bombproof hangar to shield it from prying eyes. Disembarking, Colonel Green and the princess were greeted by the commanding officer and hurried on their way. Timing was critical.

As they rode through the dark night in an unmarked car toward the United States Capitol, Colonel Green and the princess nodded off to sleep. Forty-five minutes later, Colonel Green was awakened. "We've got someone tailing us, sir," the driver informed Colonel Green. Glancing back, Colonel Green saw a black luxury car, its bright headlights glaring at them.

"Radio ahead," said Colonel Green. "Get some of your men to cut them off."

"Right," said Colonel Green's driver, picking up his radio. "Units 1 and 2," we've picked up a tailer. Black luxury car, license number OH1432. Get tractor 2 ready."

"Roger. Out."

As the two cars sped down the narrow highway at an increasing speed, a large farm tractor towing a set of discs suddenly pulled out into the road in front of them, blocking both lanes. Colonel Green's driver hit the brakes and jerked the steering wheel to avoid a collision. Their car slid off the pavement and spun around in the dirt. Tires squealing, the black luxury car fishtailed and stopped just inches behind them. Colonel Green threw open his door and, grabbing the princess' arm, said, "C'mon Princess, we're getting out of here!"

Once out of the car, they found themselves looking down the barrels of six submachine guns. The men who held the weapons were dressed in camouflaged army uniforms; a round olive drab patch with a black broccoli sprig in the middle of it adorned each man's left shoulder. "Hands up, peaceful like," ordered the men's leader.

"What do you want with us?" asked Colonel Green.

"The attaché case," replied the man. "And if you don't do what we say quickly, your *lives.*"

CHAPTER 12

Museum Mystery

Awaking from a good night's sleep, the Wright cousins ate a hearty breakfast in their plush hotel. They secured their rooms for another night and made plans for the day. While the girls worked on tracking down the cousins' missing luggage, Robert and Tim gathered up the ingredients from a nearby store and *very carefully* assembled some "top secret" Broccoli Bombs. As Tim would put it, "no self-respecting secret agent—or general citizen, for that matter—would be caught without the dreaded Broccoli Bomb. BB for short." Robert and Tim also bought some new batteries for Robert's watch.

When the girls phoned the Turtle Taxi Company, the customer service clerk said he'd had no reports of their lost luggage, but he "would definitely get back to them if it showed up."

Work done, Robert, Tim—attachés in hand—and the girls, set out for a popular nearby hands-on military history museum. They were going to play "tourist" for a while.

On the way to the museum, Lindy picked up a newspaper from off the sidewalk. "Hey guys, listen to this," she said as they strolled along. "It says here that Congress is expected to pass a bill this afternoon that will make it mandatory for every person in the United States to eat two helpings of vegetables at every meal."

"What does *mandatory* mean?" asked Tim.

"It means *forced to*, or *you have to*," Lindy replied.

"We'll have to eat vegetables at every meal?" said Tim.

"A double helping," said Lindy, skimming ahead. "And it doesn't mean carrots and corn and all the easy ones. No, they want us to eat lima beans, asparagus, and broccoli!"

"No way," said Tim.

"That's horrible," said Robert. "They can't tell us what to eat."

"They say it's for the people's health," said Lindy.

"Baloney," replied Robert. "There's something more behind it; it's some kind of power grab or money thing or something."

"It's cruel and inhumane treatment," said Tim. "That's what it is."

"Doesn't say there's been much opposition to it," continued Lindy. "People just don't seem to care anymore."

"I care," said Tim. "And if there was some way we could get word to the kids of America, they'd have a riot on their hands!"

"Yes," added Robert. "And if it did pass, we could tell all the kids to slip their lima beans, asparagus, and broccoli to their pets while their parents weren't looking."

"But then they'd get in trouble for cruelty to animals," said Tim.

"Oh, you guys are terrible," said Kimberly. "Now what's wrong with broccoli? I for one like it."

"I do, too," agreed Lindy. "Particularly fresh broccoli." Then she got a pained look on her face. "But I can't eat much of it because it bothers my stomach."

"It bothers my stomach, too," said Robert.

"Yeah," Tim agreed. "Mine, too. And it bothers my hair."

"Right," said Robert. "And my nose."

"Yeah," Tim agreed. "It bothers my stomach and my hair and my nose, too. And my eyes."

"And our ears, too," Robert added, shifting his top secret attaché case into his other hand. "And our toes."

"All right, all right, enough already," said Kimberly. "Why don't you guys admit it. I think you secret agents just don't like *broccoli.*"

"Oh yes we do," said Robert. "Just not for eating."

"Yeah," added Tim, "it makes great stink bombs."

Arriving at the museum, the four cousins saw a large sign on the front of the tan, multi-storied building. "*SWORDS & SHIELDS Military History Museum*," it proclaimed. After paying a small "contribution" entrance fee, the cousins fanned out to explore the exhibits.

There was a section on the *Realm of the Knights* with real suits of armor. Dozens of different kinds of swords, spears and other weapons were mounted on the walls. Another section—*The Bow Age*—covered earlier weapons with bows and arrows and obsidian-headed artifacts. Rifles, uniforms, and other equipment were displayed from the Revolutionary, Civil, and Spanish American Wars. Weapons and military vehicles were also displayed from World War 1, World War 2, and the Korean, Vietnam, Desert Storm, and Afghanistan Wars. There was even a display of possible futuristic equipment with robot soldiers.

"Tanks," said Tim eagerly. "Robert, they've got tanks and jeeps and armored cars!" Tim was about to climb onto one of the tanks, but Kimberly stopped him by saying, "You're probably not really supposed to touch them."

"But how can I hurt a tank?" asked Tim.

"You'd find a way," said Kimberly. "Now it's our turn. Let's go see the doll museum instead."

"Doll museum?" said Tim, scrunching up his nose.

"Yes," replied Kimberly. "I saw the *ANTIQUE DOLL AND DRESS MUSEUM* down the street. It's the big, pink building."

"Dolls? We have to go look at dolls?" said Tim. "The ones that burp and wet and cry and stuff? You're not serious, are you?"

"I hear they've got every Barbie-Q doll that was ever made," added Lindy.

"I'm gonna die," said Tim. "I'm just gonna die."

"Oh, Tim, come on. You'll like it. Just wait and see," said Kimberly.

"Yeah, Timbo," Robert added with a smile. "Um, you'll have to excuse me, I want to go see–."

"Wait a second, Robert. We wouldn't want you to miss out, too," said Lindy with a smile.

"Me?" said Robert. "But Lindy, dolls and stuff, that's torture. Why don't you and Kimberly go over there by yourselves–it's just two doors down–and we'll look around here for a little while longer. Okay?"

"Okay," Lindy said reluctantly. "We'll meet you in an hour and a half at the front door." With that, the girls left.

"Robert, thanks for saving my life," said Tim. "What do you want to see next?"

"The big tank around the corner," Robert said. "Follow me."

Robert led Tim over to a large, camouflaged vehicle with eight wheels and a turret with a cannon on the front of it. Every surface of the sleek vehicle was sloped at an angle for maximum protection.

Stopping at a display sign at the front of the vehicle, Robert and Tim read:

> 8-WHEELED ARMORED CAR: U. S. LAV-25 (Light Armored Vehicle)

Crew: 9
Armament: 25 mm automatic cannon and 7.62 mm co-axial machine gun.
8-wheel-drive
Maximum speed: Road–63 mph, Swimming–6 mph.

"That thing swims?" asked Tim, eyeing the front slope of the vehicle.

"I guess so," said Robert, walking around the side of it. "How do you think they get in it?" Reaching the back of the vehicle, Robert answered his own question. "Hey Tim," he said, "There are two big doors and some propellers back here."

"And some more hatches up here," Tim called down from the top of the vehicle. "There are two hatches on top of the turret and one down near the front. Must be for the driver." Tim pried up one of the hatches and peered inside. "Wow, this is really cool."

"Tim, what in the world are you doing up there?" asked a girl's voice. Tim dropped the hatch, barely missing his fingers. "Oh, hi, Kimberly," he said. "I was just looking–Robert and I were trying to figure out how to get inside this thing. Boy, I'd love to have something like this that swims. We could park it in the middle of Lake Magoogoo and use it as a diving board."

"What happened to the doll museum?" Robert called out from the rear of the armored car.

"Somebody locked the front doors of this museum," replied Lindy. "We can't get out."

"They locked *this* museum?" said Robert.

"What about the back door?" volunteered Tim, eager to get rid of his sister.

"It was locked, too," said Kimberly.

"That's weird," said Robert. "What about the ticket guy we saw at the front door?"

"He's gone," said Lindy. "We couldn't find anybody. They must have closed the museum for lunch or something. Robert, maybe you can figure a way out."

Tim climbed back down off the armored car and he and Robert went to investigate. Arriving at the entrance, they found everything just as the girls had said. The place seemed deserted.

"Bummer," said Tim.

"This is serious," said Kimberly. "We've got to find a way out of here."

"It could be worse," said Tim.

"How so?" asked Kimberly, placing her hands on her hips.

"We could be stuck in that pink *doll* museum."

A quick inspection of the rest of the museum gave similar results. The exterior doors were securely locked and there wasn't another soul in the whole building. Or at least, that's what it *seemed.*

CHAPTER 13

Iron Suits Me Fine

"Stuck in a war museum with a *hands-on* room," said Tim, suddenly feeling like a kid in a candy store. "I wonder what it was like in the old days to wear a suit of armor."

"Tim?" said Kimberly. "Are you thinking what I think you're thinking?"

"Well it's a *hands-on* museum, isn't it?" said Tim.

"Yes, but–."

"*Yahoo!*" shouted Tim and he ran off in the direction of the KNIGHTS IN SHINING ARMOR exhibit. Kimberly raced after Tim to make sure he didn't get into trouble.

"Hand me the other foot piece," said Tim, seated beside a suit of armor his size.

"Tim," said Kimberly, "you really shouldn't be doing this."

"Now for the breast plate," said Tim, rising to his feet. "Now the arms."

Tim was actually beginning to look like a knight in shining armor.

"I just hope we don't get into trouble," said Kimberly.

"Aw, Kimberly," Tim said. "This place is made for kids; hands-on, you saw the sign. We can try on any type of old army clothes and helmets they have in this room. Only bummer is that we can't use any of the weapons. They're all fastened to the walls for some reason." Tim tried on the knight's helmet. "How do I look?" he asked.

"Just like a can of tuna," Kimberly replied with a grin.

"Where's a mirror?" asked Tim.

"Right over here," Kimberly said, escorting him over to a nearby wall.

Tim tried walking, but nearly fell over. "Boy," he said, "this armor's heavy."

Kimberly laughed. "Open up your visor so you can see yourself better," she said.

Raising his visor, Tim was all smiles. "Boy, I can't wait–." But the visor slipped back down, making a loud squeaking sound as it did. Pushing it back up, Tim said, "I can't wait to show this to Robert." Turning to go, his suit creaked again. Tim carefully raised his visor and whispered, "I think I'll sneak up on Robert and Lindy."

Kimberly laughed and followed the squeaking, creaking knight toward the armored car. Not spying anyone at the armored car, Tim gave up his surprise attack and pounded on the vehicle's frontal armor with his gauntlet-covered hand. "Anyone home?" he called out.

A hatch on the top of the turret swung open and out popped Lindy's head, complete with goggles and tanker's helmet.

Raising his visor, Tim said, "Hi Lindy. Where's Robert?"

"In here," said Robert, raising the driver's hatch. "Hey, Sir Tim, you should see this, it's really neat. It works just like a regular car."

Tim smiled. His visor dropped with a loud squeak and he raised it back up. "You should try on one of these tin cans," he said.

"Maybe later. Check out this armored car," said Robert. "We're trying to figure out how to turn the turret."

"Hey Kimberly," Lindy called out from the top of the turret, "check this out, it's kind of fun. There's a door in the back you can climb in. And you wouldn't believe it, they even have water and food storage in this thing."

Kimberly headed for the rear of the armored car while Tim, eager to explore it himself, squeakily hurried back to the knight's exhibit to take off his armor. Nearing the Egyptian area, Tim's visor slapped down again, causing him to trip on a piece of carpet. He lost his balance and fell against a wood-paneled wall. To his surprise, the wall moved. Upon closer inspection, he found he'd knocked open a secret door.

"Wow," said Tim, cautiously peering inside. "I wonder where this goes."

Tim pushed the door open wider. But in the process, he accidentally tripped over his own iron boot and crashed headlong into the dimly lit secret room. The door slammed shut behind him with a thud. As the light disappeared, Tim thought he spied some box-shaped objects and beside them was something wrapped in ace bandages. It looked like a body, something that looked an awful lot like a–.

"Oh no!" said Tim.

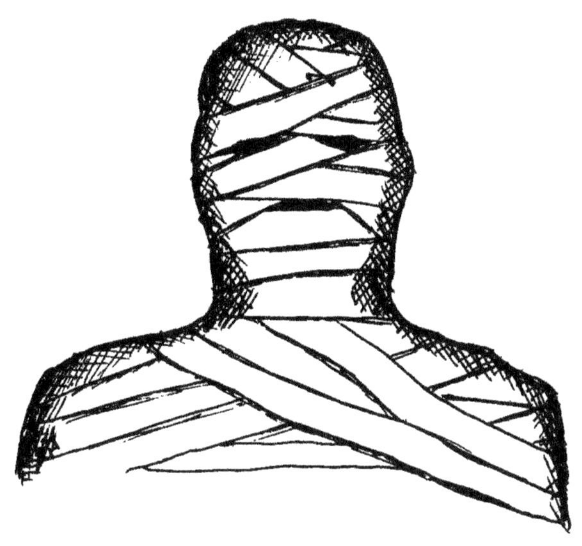

CHAPTER 14

Where's My Mummy?

Tim had watched too many scary movies and they were now coming back to haunt him in the dimly lit room. "The mummified dog!" he yelled hysterically, his voice echoing around in the iron suit.

Tim tried to scoot away but trying to get away from the mummy while wearing the suit of iron was like trying to get a burnt pancake out of a sticky frying pan. Struggling to get his hands beside his chest, Tim did a push up and managed to get to his knees. Once there, he peered around the room, trying to figure out a way to get to a standing position.

"The boxes," Tim thought. "I can push myself up on the boxes. If only they weren't so close to...the mummy. Course, I do have an iron punch," he said, tightening his right hand into a fist. "Punch," he thought, wrinkling his nose. "I wonder what a mummy feels like if you punch it? What if the mummy attacked me and I hit it and my hand went right through it? Yech!"

Finding no other way to get up, Tim decided he'd have to chance it. He cautiously scooted over to the boxes. As he did so, he caught sight of the mummy's two scary eyes staring at him. They looked so real. Tim felt his sweaty palms turn cold. "The eyes moved," Tim thought. "I know I saw them move."

Tim started to back away, but then, looking into the eyes again, he discovered that they weren't so much frightening as they were *frightened.*

"Are you...alive?" Tim asked, looking into the mummy's eyes.

The mummy nodded slowly.

"A *live* mummy? That's even worse than a dead mummy," said Tim. "I've got to get out of here."

The mummy tried to move, and Tim clanged backwards in his armor. But as he did so, he suddenly realized the mummy was trying to tell him something. Tim raised his right arm to the square. "I come in peace," he said.

The mummy nodded again.

"It's not such a bad mummy," thought Tim. "In fact, it's kind of a nice mummy. I wonder whose it is?"

The mummy struggled against its bonds, trying to speak. "Mmum-melp," it said.

"You want me to help you?" asked Tim.

The mummy nodded.

"If I help you get free, you won't kill me or anything, will you?"

The mummy shook its head "no."

Taking off his iron gauntlets, Tim began to unwrap the mummy's head. Soon, a nose appeared, and he could see the eyes better.

"Mmm-mmm," pleaded the mummy.

"Please," said Tim. "You must enunciate your words more clearly. I can tell you've never been around my great Aunt Opal."

The mummy squirmed and tried to chew its gag in half. "MUM!" hollered the mummy desperately in a muffled voice.

"HELP!" yelled Tim, his visor slamming closed with a loud squeak. "Robert, Kimberly, Lindy—somebody help!"

"Sounds like Tim hurt himself," said Kimberly, jumping down from the armored car. "Hold on, Tim," Kimberly shouted back. "We're coming to help!"

Both Tim and the mummy kept yelling, getting more frightened by the minute. Tracking the muffled noise, Kimberly led the others to the knight's exhibit area. They saw no one, but they could still hear the muffled voices.

"It sounds like it's coming from inside this wall," said Kimberly in surprise. "Now what's Timothy gotten himself into?"

Kimberly, Lindy, and Robert pushed on the wall and to their surprise, it opened. There before them in a small, hidden room were Tim and the mummy.

Tim raised his visor and pointed at the mummy. "Be careful," he said hoarsely. "That mummy told me it's a *real* mummy."

Ignoring Tim's warning, the cousins set to work helping the frightened mummy. They soon had its arms freed and as they unwrapped its head, they found it to be a girl with long, braided blond hair. They quickly removed her gag.

"Please help me," said the girl, her sweet and pleasant voice pleading. "Some men kidnapped me and put me in here."

"Sarina?" said Lindy, remembering the princess they had met at Fort Courage.

"I...I'm Katrina. Katrina Straunsee. Sarina is my twin sister."

"Princess Katrina?" said Kimberly.

Tim's visor slammed down with a loud squeak and he raised it back up to speak. "Sir Tim," he said. "Sir Tim at your service."

The cousins sped up their unwrapping. "How many were there?" asked Lindy.

"Four or five, I think. This place is their headquarters. They wore uniforms with a broccoli patch on their shoulders. They are some kind of anti-American group. Please hurry."

"Oh for a pair of scissors," said Lindy.

"I've got a pocketknife," said Robert, digging into his front pocket. Opening his knife, he began cutting through the layers of bandage.

"Careful not to cut her," cautioned Kimberly.

The cousins soon had Katrina's arms free so she could help in getting her legs unbound. The princess's legs were stiff and swollen.

"Can you walk?" asked Kimberly.

"I must," Katrina replied.

"Good, let's get out of here," said Robert, closing his knife.

The three cousins lifted Katrina to her feet and helped her take a short step.

"Hey, what about me?" called out Tim.

"Don't worry, Tim, we'll come back for you," said Robert.

"No way," said Tim clanking to his feet. "I'm not staying in here. I'm coming with you."

"Then let's go," said Robert.

Robert and Lindy stood on each side of Katrina, put her arms over their shoulders in a fireman's carry, and helped her out of the secret room. Kimberly helped Tim. They headed for the front doors of the museum. As they neared the large, plate glass doors, Princess Katrina stiffened.

"What's wrong?" asked Lindy.

"Those men across the street are the ones that kidnapped me!"

"Oh wow," said Tim, his visor clanging shut as he brought up the rear. "What do we do now?"

"Try the back door," said Robert.

"Right," said Lindy.

The cousins hurried to the back door, only to see more of the kidnappers approaching.

"What *is* this?" said Tim. "Some kind of kidnappers' convention?"

"Where to now?" asked Kimberly.

"The armored car," said Robert. "And hurry!"

CHAPTER 15

Trapped!

Arriving at the armored car, the cousins opened the rear doors and climbed inside. They almost had to use a can opener on Tim, but they finally got all the armor off him and hid it under the armored car. That done, the cousins closed the rear doors and held a quick huddle with the princess. Kimberly gave Katrina a few granola bars and a small juice box from her purse to renew her strength.

"Please," pleaded Princess Katrina as she hungrily ate, "there is not much time. We have worked so hard to get to America. The evil men...the authorities...they have taken my friend and the attaché case somewhere–."

Tears began flowing down Katrina's cheeks and she hid her face in her hands.

"Do you know where, Katrina?" asked Lindy.

"No," said the princess. "Please don't let the men capture me again. I had hoped we would be safe on our F121 plane."

"F121?" said Robert.

"Yes, we flew on F121," replied Princess Katrina. "But it did no good. Even though we could outrun the planes, we could not outrun the black sedan."

"You were chased by planes?" asked Robert, puzzled.

"Many planes," said Katrina.

"How many?" asked Robert.

"Come on, Robert," said Kimberly. "We've got to figure out how we're going to get out of here."

"Wait. Princess Katrina," Robert asked again, "how many planes were there?"

"Ten."

"Hey, that's just like in our video game last night," said Tim.

"And you had an attaché case?" asked Robert. "A top secret one like this?"

Robert set down his top secret attaché case, accidentally hitting a hidden button. A voice recording suddenly spoke out loudly:

"Welcome, Kimosoggy and Toronto..."

Robert bear-hugged his case to try to muffle it.

"As America's top two secret agents..." the voice continued, **"the President of the United States of America has assigned you an urgent mission. This is a Top Secret, Priority Alpha Mission. T.S.P.A.M. for short. Your T-SPAM is to locate and secure Princess Katrina and the attaché case, no matter the cost. If you fail, there will be dire consequences at home and abroad. America's future security is depending on you. YOU MUST NOT FAIL!"**

Princess Katrina looked at the cousins. "Who *are* you guys?" she asked with wonder.

Robert took one look at his briefcase and then back at Katrina. "We're them," Robert said. "They think we're them."

"Who?" said Tim.

"Kimosoggy and Toronto," Robert replied, dumbfounded.

"We're them. They think we're us. That T-SPAM thing...the spy stuff is for *real.*"

"The bomb at the airport, the money, the airplane game," said Tim. "They're not spoofs? And us? We're supposed to be America's top two secret agents? You Kimosoggy, me Toronto? Robert, you're talking about major, big-league stuff."

"And the President of the United States is counting on us," said Robert.

"Well," said Tim, "maybe the president can't count too well, because I'm still only fourteen, and that makes me a *minor* in *any* state. We're going to get creamed!"

"No, you are doing well," said Katrina encouragingly. "You already found me. We just need to find my pilot and the attaché case."

"But we don't even know your pilot's name," said Tim.

"It's Mr. Green," said Princess Katrina, "Mr. Steve Green."

"Steve Green?" said Lindy in surprise.

"Yes, do you know him?"

"We ought to," Lindy replied, "he's our uncle."

"They've got Uncle Steve?" said Tim. "Those dirty rotten creepazoids can't do that! Let's go find him!"

CHAPTER 16

Museum Mess-up

"Katrina," asked Lindy, "do you know where they've got Uncle Steve?"

"No. They split us up," the princess replied. "I think the attaché case must be with him, though. They were very eager to get into it."

"Okay," said Robert, "then we'll search this museum for Uncle Steve. Katrina, you'd better stay in here, out of sight. We don't want them to get you again. Kimberly, maybe you can stay with her. The rest of us will look around. If anything goes wrong, Tim and I will try to keep open the path of escape by using *Emergency Plan PC*, creating a whole lot of *Panic and Confusion*."

Robert handed out secret agent button radios from his attaché case to Lindy and Kimberly. They switched their radios onto monitor mode. Just as they were about to climb out of the armored car, they heard rapid footsteps and shouting outside. Robert motioned for silence and he and Tim slipped quietly up into the turret. Each climbed onto a turret ring seat and peered out the periscopes surrounding the hatches above them.

"What do you see?" whispered Kimberly.

"There are two men at the front of the armored car," Robert whispered back.

"What are they doing?"

"Talking," said Tim. "But I can't hear what they're saying. Robert climbed down from the turret and moved forward into the driver's area of the armored car. With great care, he propped open his hatch, ever so slightly, so he could hear their conversation. "I saw two kids run over this way," one of the men said.

Robert tried to brace his arms and accidentally knocked loose an adjustable wrench. It clanged loudly to the floor of the armored car.

"Did you hear that?" asked one of the men in front of the armored car.

"Yes," said the second man, motioning toward the armored car. "It sounded like it came from over there."

The two men eyed the camouflaged vehicle suspiciously. The second man lifted a radio to his lips. "Porcupine 1, this is Porcupine 2. We think the intruders are on the first floor. We've posted guards at both entrances and chained the doors. They won't get away, sir."

"I'll be right there. Over," said Porcupine 1.

Wincing, Robert eased his hatch down. "Nobody move," he whispered. "They're coming our way. They must have discovered we've got Katrina."

Lindy heard static on the miniature button radio Robert had given her. Picking it up, she heard a click followed by several audible tones. "Somebody's making a phone call," she whispered. "Hey Robert, I shouldn't be able to hear phone calls on this thing, should I?"

"Beats me," Robert whispered back. "I've never used these radios before."

"Rats," said Lindy, now hearing only silence. "I think they just hung up."

Glued to their periscopes, Robert and Tim saw the two men walk around the sides of the armored car. "If they spot the knight's armor," whispered Robert, "we're in for it."

"Keep your eyes peeled," said the man with the radio. "They could be anywhere around here."

"What's going on, Porcupine 2?" came a third voice. The newcomer was Porcupine 1.

"We heard a noise over here, sir," said Porcupine 2. "We've got everything locked down, sir. We'll find the princess. But don't you think you should call to let the boss know she's escaped?"

"Not yet," said Porcupine 1 bitterly. "How did she escape? You had her tied securely, didn't you?"

"Yes sir. There was no possible way she could have gotten loose."

"Then she must have had help," said Porcupine 1. "And you're sure she hasn't made it out of the building?"

"Yes sir," replied Porcupine 2. "One of our men saw she and another girl on a security camera. He's sure it was the princess. We got the doors secured before they had a chance to get out."

"Good," said Porcupine 1."

"Sir, we'd better call and let the boss know," said Porcupine 2. "If he finds out the princess is gone and we didn't tell him—."

"All right, all right, don't push me," said Porcupine 1. "But I don't see what your big worry is. You said yourself we've confined the princess."

Porcupine 1 stared at his cell phone with a sour look on his face and slowly began to dial.

Hearing the dial tones, Lindy held up her radio for all to hear.

"Badger, this is Porcupine 1," the museum leader said.

"Yes?"

"Sir, I am calling to report that we have misplaced the *package.*"

"What?! Porcupine 1, you were instructed to hold the package as hostage until we extracted the attaché opening information from Mr. Green here. Your failure is inexcusable."

"I understand, sir, but we are positive the princess is still in the museum. We have sealed off all exits."

"Good," replied Badger. "See that she does not escape. If you must, destroy the museum, you hear? I want no more foul-ups. And when you find the princess, terminate her! We're going to do the same with Green as soon as he tells us what we want."

Shocked, Porcupine 1 resisted. "Sir," he said, "killing the princess was not part of the bargain."

"Porcupine 1," threatened Badger. "There must be no trace of the princess's presence in America. You will carry out my orders exactly as I have said. Oh, and Porcupine 1, you have made two mistakes already. Once more, and your charming American wife will find herself a widow. Out."

"Out," said Porcupine 1, grimacing as he switched off his phone. Up until this point, Porcupine 1 had gone along with the Badger's demands. Porcupine 1 had gathered information about top secret U.S. military projects and passed it along. It had almost seemed harmless and he had been well paid for it. But for some time now, he'd had an uneasy feeling. While he shaved in the morning, he could no longer look himself in the eye and feel comfortable.

Porcupine 1 had grown to like living in America. It was far different from his native country, and most of the American people had been kind toward him. He liked being able to go to the grocery store and actually find food there, not like in his country back home. Why, he could even travel from city to city without secret police following him. Porcupine 1 had not realized it before, but he was beginning to *enjoy* this American freedom. Had he chosen the wrong side to fight for? The government *should* control every decision in a person's life, shouldn't it? He wasn't so sure anymore. Did he really want to see the entire world *enslaved* under his dictator's iron fist?

"And what of the millions of Americans who must be slaughtered in the process?" he thought. "Americans who would only be fighting to keep their right to own property, live their religions, and raise their families as they chose. He was beginning to think he didn't want their blood on his hands after all.

Porcupine 1 recoiled at the thought of what he had just been asked to do. He did not want to murder the innocent young Princess Katrina. But if he didn't, he himself would be killed. "If only there was some way out," he thought with an uneasy sigh.

"Come on, Porcupine 2," Porcupine 1 said bitterly. "We have dirty work to do. Let's go find that princess."

The three men continued past the armored car to the displays beyond.

Within the armored car, the speechless cousins looked at Katrina and then at each other. Robert was the first to speak. "Don't worry, Katrina," he whispered solemnly. "We'll get you out."

"We all will," Lindy whispered. "And we'll find Uncle Steve, too."

"What can we do?" asked Kimberly. "We don't even know where he is. And they've got guns."

"Oh, ye of little faith," said Lindy with a slight smile. "Just get me to a phone and we'll track them down."

"What good will that do?" asked Kimberly.

"Oh Kimberly, don't be such a pessimist," Lindy replied. "I memorized the phone number they just called."

"You did what?" said Kimberly.

"Memorized the phone number," said Lindy. "It's easy. Once you know which numbers go to which tones, you've got it made!"

"That's my sis," Robert whispered proudly with a smile. "And we can track the phone number to a physical address. Now, to get out of the museum."

"Maybe we can disguise ourselves as newspaper delivery boys," suggested Tim. "And wear fake noses with eyeglasses."

"This is no time for joking," reprimanded Kimberly.

"Who's joking," said Tim. "Nobody, but nobody recognizes you in those things. And we could use our Broccoli Bombs."

"You and your Broccoli Bombs," said Kimberly. "Tim, this is serious."

While the rest of the cousins continued their brainstorming, Robert's mind wandered to the driving controls in front of him. "Boy, if we only had an armored car like this that could really work. Now *that* would be awesome."

Toying with a main electrical switch, Robert accidentally flipped it on. The dashboard lit up. "That's odd," he thought. On a hunch, Robert tapped the starter switch and heard the starter solenoid click.

"No way," he said, hardly able to contain his growing excitement. "This thing isn't operational, is it? And yet the fuel, oil pressure, and amp gauges all seem to work."

Robert tapped the starter switch and heard it click again. "Hey guys," he whispered excitedly, "this vehicle isn't a de-militarized model. *This armored car really works!*"

CHAPTER 17

The Great Escape

"What?" whispered Tim, peering down from up in the turret.

"At least the electrical system works," replied Robert. "And the fuel gage moved, so it must have fuel. I wonder what they were going to use it for?"

"Maybe it's their getaway car," said Tim.

"Oh Robert," Lindy whispered excitedly. "Do you really think so? It would be an answer to our prayers!"

"See," said Robert, switching on the rest of the armored car's interior lights. "Help me find a manual on how to drive this thing."

The cousins immediately began searching the interior of the armored car. Digging through a pouch next to his seat, Robert discovered a booklet for the vehicle. "OPERATOR'S MANUAL FOR LIGHT ARMORED VEHICLE: 8x8, M1047," it said on the cover. He quickly handed it to Lindy, asking her to scan it while he familiarized himself with the instruments and controls. "Tim, keep your eyes open and let us know if we have any more company."

Locating the starting and driving sections, Lindy knelt behind Robert and quickly helped him go through the process of how to start and drive the vehicle.

Kimberly and Katrina found and handed out tanker's helmets to each person in the armored car.

"Hey, these things have radios," said Robert, adjusting his helmet. "We'll be able to talk to each other. Let's get out of here!"

Everyone quickly strapped themselves into their various seats—Robert in the front, Tim in the turret, and Lindy, Kimberly, and Princess Katrina in the back troop passenger area.

"Everybody set?" said Robert, looking out his periscopes. A nervous shiver of excitement ran down his spine.

"Yes," came four replies.

"Okay," said Robert, speaking softly over his headset, "Let's go."

Checking through his periscopes to make sure nobody was around, Robert pressed the pre-heat switch. "Look out, world," Robert whispered with a grin, "Cause the Wright Cousins are about to roll!"

When the engine light turned from red to green, Robert switched on the starter. ***Rup-rup-rup*** grumbled the engine. He cranked it again. "The batteries must be low," he whispered.

Rup-rup-**rup** went the engine again, its sound echoing through the museum. The engine slowed. Robert had to let off the starter to keep it from burning out. Shouting could be heard in the distance.

"Robert, hurry up," said Kimberly.

Robert cranked the large engine again. "Come on, come on," he said imploringly.

"Somebody's in the armored car," shouted a voice.

"Robert, hurry up," said Kimberly.

"Five guys just rounded the corner—they're headed our way," reported Tim. "And they've got machine guns," he added in a whining voice.

"Lock all the hatches and doors," ordered Robert.

Robert and Tim's eyes were glued to the periscopes. "Here they come," said Tim. "There are three more behind us."

Robert tried the starter again. The starter was cranking more slowly as it drained the power from the batteries. ***Rup—rup—rup-rup***. The cousins' hearts sank. There was a loud thump as two of the men reached the armored car and leapt onto its frontal armor.

"They're on the front," shouted Tim. Seconds later there was clanging at the back of the vehicle as another man hammered on the door latch.

"Robert, do something!" said Kimberly.

"I'm trying," Robert replied. He cranked the starter again, and with each crank the interior lights flickered dimmer.

The rear door latch started to turn. Kimberly and Katrina leapt to hold it. ***Rup—rup-rup*** went the engine.

A third man was now on the front of the vehicle. Lindy grabbed the latch of the other rear door. "Tim, help us!" she called out.

Lindy, Kimberly and Katrina were struggling to keep the rear doors closed. Kimberly's door was being pulled open. A hand reached in. Kimberly and Katrina punched it away and pulled the door closed.

Rup—Rup-Rup. The armored car shuddered as thick, black smoke began to pour out of its exhaust pipe. The engine caught and suddenly roared to life.

"Yahoo!" exclaimed Robert, shifting the transmission into drive. He stepped on the throttle and with a menacing roar, the massive armored car leapt forward. "Let's get out of here!" said Robert

Outside the armored car, Porcupine's men fell all over each other trying to get out of the way. Two still clung to the top of the vehicle, but they dove off as their comrades' bullets began to ping off the vehicle's armor.

"Turn more to the left," Tim shouted down to Robert.

Too late, Robert turned the steering wheel as the vehicle smashed through the corner of the secret room and ripped it wide open.

"Oh mummy," exclaimed Tim. "That was great. I like this armored car already!"

They reached the main corridor and turned sharply.

"They've blocked the entrance with a Humvee army truck," Tim announced excitedly, "and they've got a bunch of guys with machine guns."

"That does it," said Robert, "I hate to do this to a nice Humvee, but they're asking for it. No more Mr. Nice Guy."

With a loud ***SMASH!*** the armored car hit the Humvee and shoved it against the doorway walls. Amidst a horrible, metallic crunching sound, the armored car drove over the top of the Humvee and slammed through the museum's front wall. Glass, bricks, and wood went flying in every direction.

Hearing a loud noise, people along the street looked up to see the armored car come smashing out through the front of the building, skid across the sidewalk, and take a sharp right turn down the street.

"The parade!" people shouted jubilantly. Grabbing up their ready-made protest signs and posters, hundreds of people, ever ready to join in a wild cause, dashed out into the street. "Follow the leader," they shouted, breaking into a run. "The parade has begun! Follow that armored car thing!"

Back in the museum, Porcupine 1 gaped at the flattened Humvee and the massive hole in the museum's front wall. "What a mess," said Porcupine 2 from behind him. "Better call the boss and let him know."

"Strike three and I'm out," said Porcupine 1. He raised his cell phone high above his head and slammed it to the floor. "You call him, Porcupine 2," he said, "I'm sick of this disgusting work."

"Hey, wait a minute," said Porcupine 2. "You can't just leave."

Porcupine 1 didn't stop to respond. He was already over the smashed Humvee and heading for the great outdoors.

"Where are you going?" yelled Porcupine 2. "The boss will never let you get away with this."

"I don't care. I've been stupid, but I'm no murderer," called back Porcupine 1, tearing the broccoli patch off his sleeve. "Even if I must go to prison, at least by defecting to the Americans' side, my family and I will have a chance. That's more than Veep would ever give me."

CHAPTER 18

Race Against Time

Two blocks away, the cousins in their armored car were stopped by a red traffic light. Robert and Tim cautiously raised their hatches and peered out.

"There's a bunch of people following us," Tim announced over the armored car's intercom. "I don't think they're from the museum."

"Do they have weapons?" asked Robert.

"No, worse," said Tim. "They've got picket signs!"

The closest people were carrying a wide banner which said:

FIRST ANNUAL NATIONAL FUN "*HEY, PAY ATTENTION TO ME!*" MARCH

"Wait a second, I know those guys," said Tim. They sent me an e-mail wanting me to be in their parade. This is their fifth year doing it."

"We're not just in it," said Robert. "It looks like we're leading it."

Dozens of people stepped from the sidewalks and fell in behind the armored car. Signs and posters sprang up all over protesting this or that thing. Signs like:

WHO SAID MUSTARD CAUSES BAD BREATH?!

STAR TREK IS *REAL!*
HI MOM!

EARTHQUAKES ARE VICTIMS, TOO–IT'S NOT THEIR FAULT!

Just when the parade people were getting uncomfortably close to the armored car, the traffic light turned green and the cousins were off.

"Come back, come back," shouted the people, breaking into a run after the armored car.

"Those people are cuckoos," said Tim, ducking his head down in the turret. "Robert, hurry and get us out of here."

As the cousins approached the next stoplight, it also turned red. Waiting for the light to change, a man pulled up beside them on a loud, highly chromed motorcycle.

"Hey, *cool SUV*," called up the motorcycle rider between the *rumble-rumbles* of his bike. "Like the camo job."

"Thanks," said Tim, casually waving down to him from the top of the turret. "We're just taking it for a spin to see if we like it."

When the light turned green, the motorcyclist revved up his bike and waved. "Enjoy," he said, starting to pull away from the line. Robert floored the armored car and left him in the dust.

The next light turned red just as they were approaching it. "Rats," said Tim, noting a pedestrian crossing the street, "I bet that guy was the one that made it turn red."

The pedestrian stopped right in front of the cousins' armored car to snap a picture of it.

"Excuse me, sir, but we're really in a hurry," called out Robert.

"Just one more picture," replied the photographer.

"Jonathan? My cousin?" said Robert, recognizing the voice. The photographer looked up in surprise. Robert stood up through his hatchway. "What are you doing here?"

"Robert?" replied Jonathan.

The light turned green and cars were starting to honk.

"Hurry up and climb on," said Robert. "We've got a bunch of cars behind us. We can talk in a minute."

"I'll take care of the horns" said Tim with a mischievous grin. He pushed a button that made the armored car's turret begin to turn.

"Tim?" said Jonathan, climbing onto the front of the armored car. "You've got Tim in the turret? Tim, what are you doing?"

"I'm gonna stop those noisy cars from honking."

"No, Tim, don't do it!" called out Jonathan, scrambling up onto the turret. Tim was just lowering the cannon barrel when Jonathan grabbed his arms through the open hatchway.

"Aw, Jonathan," Tim complained. "I wasn't really gonna fire at them, just give them a scare. We don't have any bullets, anyways."

"Tim, move over and let me in," Jonathan said. Just then, Robert stepped on the gas pedal to go and Jonathan nearly fell through the turret hatch headfirst.

"Jonathan, how did you get here?" asked Kimberly. "I thought you were in the hospital!"

"I guess I ruined the surprise," said Jonathan, rubbing his shoulder once he was inside the armored car. "Dad had a lot of frequent flyer miles saved up, so he and Mom and I were going to surprise you guys at Tim's poetry recital tonight."

Jonathan continued, "Mom and Dad are at the airport

trying to track down our lost luggage. You know, that crazy hospital got my records mixed up with somebody else's. They were getting ready to do an open-heart surgery on me. You should see the cutting lines they had drawn on my chest."

"Meet our new friend," said Lindy, smiling as she gestured toward princess Katrina.

Jonathan froze when he saw the princess. "Sarina?" he said in amazement, reaching out to take her hand. Katrina blushed slightly and smiled.

"Oh, no, wait," said Kimberly, "Jonathan, this is Katrina, Sarina's identical twin sister. Princess Katrina, this is my older brother, Jonathan."

"Oh, hi," said Jonathan, shaking her hand. "Katrina, you've got deep blue-green eyes, too. Goodness, you sure look like your sister."

"It is nice to finally meet you," said Katrina. "My sister has told me so many wonderful things about you since her visit to America."

"We just rescued Katrina from the museum," Robert called back from the driver's seat. "We're on our way to rescue Uncle Steve. Maybe you can take over driving this thing so Lindy and I can locate him."

"Sure," said Jonathan, "anything I can do to help. Katrina, I'm so glad you're safe."

Robert pulled into a parking lot and stopped the large vehicle. "Okay," he said, glancing at his watch. "Lindy, what was that Badger guy's phone number again? Let's find his address."

Lindy told Robert the number and Robert punched it into his watch. After a moment, the address appeared on his watch's display. "It's a residence at 3450 Maple Way," he said. "Do we need the guy's social security number and what kind of car he drives?"

"Sure," said Lindy. "Let's make a file on him."

"Does it tell when he last went to the dentist?" asked Tim.

"No," Robert replied with a chuckle, "but he drives a black luxury car and he has two dogs. His place is way out in the country."

"How do we get there?" asked Jonathan.

"This armored car is equipped with electronic maps," said Lindy. "I glanced at the manual."

"Lindy," Jonathan said with a smile, "All I can say is I'm glad you're on *our* side."

The cousins quickly pulled out the armored car's navigation table and punched Badger's address into its computer. A map appeared on the display, pinpointing the location of the address.

"It's a medium-sized house with an attached garage," said Lindy, studying an enlarged image of the property. "There's an expressway that goes by about three miles to the north of it. They may be expecting us."

"I was just thinking the same thing," said Robert. "We'll need my watch to see what's going on."

"I'll drive, you watch," said Jonathan. "No pun intended."

They found Jonathan a helmet equipped with radio. He quickly settled into the driver's seat as Robert showed him the different controls. "Just like a truck," said Jonathan.

"More top-heavy," Robert said. "That turret weighs a lot, so it leans a little to the outside when you turn. Be careful of that."

Robert climbed up into the turret with Tim and opened the hatch above him.

"Everybody set?" called out Jonathan over the intercom headsets.

"Yes," came five replies.

"We're on our way," called back Jonathan, glancing at the dash and eyeing the electronic map. "We'll cut across the park next to us and hit the main drag. That should save us a lot of time."

"But it's hilly," replied Kimberly. "We might get stuck."

"Sis," said Jonathan with a grin. "This is an 8-wheel-drive, four-wheel-steering armored car. Somehow, I don't think we're going to have a problem."

"And it swims, too," added Tim.

"Cool," said Jonathan. "But let's not cross the Atlantic just yet."

Emerging from the other side of the park, Jonathan pulled out onto a street heading east. Once again, they were stopped by two red lights in a row.

"That does it," said Robert, "no more Mr. Nice Guy. Tim, get our secret agent attaché glasses and clear the decks for action."

"You mean like the airplane game?" Tim said excitedly.

"Exactly," said Robert. "Break out the specs."

Robert and Tim put on their sunglasses and tapped the on switch in the right frame. Red crosshairs appeared in the lenses. Pushing a button on his wristwatch, Robert brought up a Heads-Up Display—HUD—on the status of the armored car they were riding in.

"Nuts," said Robert. "We're out of cannon ammunition."

"Maybe we could use our Broccoli Bombs," said Tim.

"Not on lights," Robert replied. "They're only anti-personnel. Wait a second, maybe there's another way. Tim, let's try locking all these rippin' stoplights on green and keep them that way."

Punching earnestly and precisely on his wristwatch, Robert typed in a new command and pressed "enter." Suddenly, every stoplight for as far as the cousins could see turned green.

"Okay Jonathan," Robert announced gleefully over their intercom. "You're clear to go!"

"Great. Now for some headlights," said Jonathan, reaching for the light switch on the armored car's dash. He accidentally hit another switch, immediately setting off a loud siren. Cars ahead in both lanes began pulling off the street to let the armored car go through.

"I still think we should have used the Broccoli Bombs," Tim said to Robert as they sped down the road in the armored car.

"Not yet," said Robert. "Let's save those for the *real* bad guys."

CHAPTER 19

Threats

Pulling onto the expressway, the cousins finally had a chance to see what the armored car could do. And do it did. It roared down the road at sixty-three miles per hour in eight-wheel-drive. Trees whipped by.

Weaving in and out of traffic, the cousins sped toward their Uncle Steve, their minds filled with all kinds of questions: What kind of enemy were they up against? How many were there? Would they arrive in time?

With traffic thinning, Jonathan switched off the siren. Because of the smooth road, the girls decided to get some fresh air and light. Opening the two hatches in the roof above them, they stood on their bench seats and surveyed the surrounding countryside. Compared to the dim confines of the armored car, the sun lifted their spirits and warmed them.

Lindy continued monitoring the button radio Robert had given her. She soon heard some noise. Someone was dialing Badger's number again! The signal was very staticky. Lindy placed the small radio up against her helmet mouthpiece so all in the armored car could hear.

"But Veep, we've got him in the garage. We're trying to extract–."

"Forget it, Badger. Somebody's just blown our whole museum front open, literally and figuratively. I can't afford to...at this time...definite."

"But we just need a little more time," replied Badger. "We're close to...evacuation to...Air Force...late...try for more."

"Negative, Badger. Just clear...don't...princess has escaped..."

"What?" asked Badger. "Why wasn't I informed? I'll get Porcupine 1 if it's the last thing I do."

"Never mind that," said Veep. "Just get rid of your package...deal with...later. You might have some company...give them a warm reception."

The signal faded, interrupted by a nearby electric transformer station. By the time the cousins' armored car cleared the interference, the phone conversation was over.

Kimberly started to panic. "Well, they know about us, and that 'warm reception' they talked about was for us. If we go in there, they're going to kill us."

"And what about Uncle Steve," Robert shot back. "We can't just leave him there."

"Let's call the police or the FBI or something," said Kimberly.

"Fine, find a phone and do that," Jonathan replied. "But they couldn't deploy in time. We're going in. You heard the phone call."

Kimberly started to protest, but Jonathan cut her off. "Kim, there are some dirty rotten scumbags that have Uncle Steve and they're about to kill him. If you want off, just say the word; I'll let you off at a call box."

"But we can't just go in 'over the top'," said Kimberly. "We'll be killed."

"That's the chance we take," said Jonathan. "But right now, we're the only chance Uncle Steve has got. We're going in, and we're going in fast. Lindy, how long till we get there?"

"About another four minutes. But we might be able to shave off a little time if we go cross-country."

"Let's go for the cross-country route," said Robert. "They might not expect us that way."

"Just tell me when to turn," said Jonathan.

Lindy glanced at the map. "There's a big water tank up ahead on the right, turn just after that."

"But there's no off-ramp," said Kimberly. "And there's a fence. It'll pop our tires."

"Kim," said Lindy. "Page 35 of the manual says we've got run flat tires. Even if they're punctured, they still won't go flat."

"But what about the wire?" asked Kimberly. "We may get stuck in it."

"Kimberly-Kim-Kim," said Jonathan. "This is an *armored car.* Armored cars are *made* to go through fences and trees. I see the water tank. Okay everybody, make sure you're strapped in. We're about to turn."

Jonathan steered the armored car to the right. It left the expressway, snapping posts and wire alike as it plowed through the "keep-the-critters-off-the-road" fence. At the top of the embankment, the armored car jumped a brow ditch and flew through the air. With a *phoompf,* it touched back down and sped into the field beyond.

"Jonathan, there should be a road up ahead," informed Lindy. "Turn right onto it."

"I see it," said Jonathan, stepping on the throttle.

"Follow the road," said Lindy. "It'll take us right to Badger's place. It dead-ends in his neighbor's front yard."

Up in the turret, Robert and Tim had been busy, too. Robert had located floor plans of the buildings on Badger's property with his watch and had downloaded them onto the secret agent glasses for he and Tim to view. Tim noticed a warning light flashing on his glasses. "Robert," he said.

"Just a second, Tim, I'm trying to locate Uncle Steve on the house security system."

"But Robert," Tim said more urgently.

"Hold on," said Robert.

"But somebody's just targeted us," said Tim.

Robert looked at his sunglasses and saw the word DANGER flashing in bright red letters. "You're right," he said. "Somebody's trying to get us. Um, let's see."

Robert tapped his glasses twice, activating an overhead view of the terrain in front of them. "Identify threats," Robert typed into his wristwatch. Several red brackets suddenly appeared on Robert and Tim's glasses. Beside the brackets appeared the words "TOW Missile Launcher."

"No way," said Robert. "That's not fair. They're not supposed to have artillery like that!"

CHAPTER 20

To the Rescue!

"What's a TOW missile?" asked Tim.

"Target-On-Wire, or something like that," replied Robert. "It's a very accurate missile."

"It looks like there are four of them," said Tim.

"We'll have to take them one at a time," said Robert, taking a deep breath. "Jonathan," he said into his microphone. "Somebody's targeting us. Try swerving a little bit, we've got to take evasive action."

"Okay," said Jonathan. "But those trees don't give us much room."

"Deactivate TOW Launcher," Robert typed. The threat brackets disappeared from their screen.

The TOW missile crews were having a terrible time. Each time they would "acquire" their target, Robert would deactivate their launchers and they would have to switch them on all over again. It was a game of who could be the fastest, but Robert had a gnawing feeling he was losing ground. One missile hit, and they'd be out of commission.

Badger, the boss of the crooks at the military museum, and his lieutenant were perched on the roof of Badger's house peering over the ridge at the cousins' swerving armored car.

"Who are those guys?" Badger asked, looking through his binoculars.

"I don't know, sir," replied the lieutenant. "But they're good."

"Well, tell your men to hurry up and launch their missiles," ordered Badger.

"Open fire!" radioed the lieutenant.

The cousins had just reached the halfway point and passed the TOW launchers that the enemy had parked on the side of the road in the bushes. The TOW crews were scrambling to get their equipment back into firing order and re-aim. To add to their pressure, they now had Badger's house and property to worry about blowing up if they missed and overshot the armored car.

"Jonathan, when you get to the tee in the road, turn left," directed Lindy. "Badger's house will be the first one on the right."

"Okay," said Jonathan.

"I've got a locator on Uncle Steve," Robert said excitedly. "I broke into Badger's home surveillance system. I've got video of Uncle Steve. They've got him tied up on the floor against the right-hand wall of the two-car garage."

"Is he okay?" asked Kimberly.

"He's still alive," said Robert.

"Thank goodness," said Kimberly.

"We'll be there in thirty seconds," informed Jonathan. "Lindy, where's the garage?"

"Just past the house."

"Robert," Tim broke in. "They've got another launcher up."

"Right, I'll get it," Robert replied, madly typing away.

Reaching the intersection, Jonathan yanked the steering wheel hard to the left. The armored car skidded around the corner and went into a slide. A TOW missile swooshed by, missing the armored car by inches. It impacted on the front right corner of Badger's rock house.

Kaboom! The missile exploded, ripping a large hole in Badger's living room. The concussion knocked Badger and the lieutenant from their feet and sent them sliding toward the roof's edge. Badger's living room now had air conditioning!

"There's the garage," said Robert. "They've got the doors closed."

Jonathan turned toward the garage. Halfway there, he accidentally hit Badger's black luxury sedan and flattened it. "Brace yourselves," warned Jonathan as he aimed for the left garage door. "We're going through."

With a loud ***Crunch,*** the armored car punched through the door without a shudder. Jonathan jammed on the brakes and brought the vehicle to a screeching halt. "Get Uncle Steve!" he called out.

Katrina and the cousins swung open the back doors and leapt out to get Uncle Steve. Grabbing him by his arms and legs, they carried and loaded him into the rear of the armored car. Katrina grabbed the attaché case from a nearby table and piled in after them.

"Let's get out of here!" called out Robert, slamming the doors shut behind them. Bullets began hitting the rear of the armored car almost immediately.

Letting off the brake, Jonathan threw the vehicle into gear and stepped on the throttle. ***Smack!*** In his hurry to leave, he mistook forward for reverse and sent the armored car crashing through the back wall of the garage.

Seeing the armored car burst into his backyard, Badger, still on the house roof, shouted commands at his lieutenant. "Stop them! Stop them!" he shouted. Snatching an MP5 submachine gun out of his lieutenant's hands, Badger turned it on the cousins' retreating armored car and opened fire.

KaBOOM! A second TOW missile found its mark, this time on Badger's garage, blowing it into a ball of flame. Badger and his lieutenant were thrown from the roof and landed in the backyard.

"Oh no," said Badger, soot-faced and glancing dazedly at the destruction around him. "And I just cancelled my homeowner's insurance!"

CHAPTER 21

Reunion

"Yahoo!" shouted Tim as they cleared the woods behind Badger's house and sped for the expressway. Everyone in the armored car immediately joined in the excitement. "We did it!" they called out, and all began talking at once. Kimberly, Lindy, and Princess Katrina helped to untie Uncle Steve.

"Princess Katrina," said Steve, "I'm so glad you're okay." He noticed his surroundings. "Where on earth did you guys get this armored car?" he asked. "And where's Aunt Opal?"

Laughter broke out, washing away all their anxiety and fears. All, that is, except Tim's, for he had noticed the time on Robert's watch. "Oh wow," he said, bumping his helmet on the steel ceiling. "I almost forgot; I've got to get to my poem recital. The President's going to be there!"

Kimberly and Tim quickly explained to Katrina and Uncle Steve about Tim's winning the PoemNet contest.

"The U.S. President will be there?" Steve asked with interest. He nodded to the princess. "We'll give him the attaché case."

"Yes," said Katrina, "and Robert, if I give you my father's contact number, would you please use your watch and let him know that I am safe?"

"Be glad to," Robert replied with a smile. "I'm glad we found you."

"Me too," said Katrina, returning the smile, "and thank you."

Kimberly located the recital hall on the electronic map. "Tim," she said. "I'm afraid you're going to have to stay in the clothes you're wearing. We don't have time to stop by the hotel."

"That's fine with me," said Tim. "I like wearing tennis shoes."

"We should be there in about ten minutes," said Jonathan.

The three girls—Kimberly, Lindy, and Katrina—looked at each other and suddenly panicked. "Our hair!" they said in distress.

Kimberly started digging through her purse. "All I've got with me are three hair ties and some bobby pins," she said.

"I can braid," Katrina volunteered. "But I could have done wonders with my professional salon spray."

"There's a mirror in the armored car's emergency kit," said Lindy. "Robert, can we borrow the comb on your multitool, please?"

The girls set to work.

Jonathan, meanwhile, drove as close as he dared to the recital hall with the armored car and parked in a pre-arranged, secure garage. Washington, D.C., was not used to having armored cars driving on its streets. Using his watch, Robert scheduled a stretched limousine to pick them up so they could arrive at the recital hall in style. Everyone enjoyed the limousine immensely and, of course, Robert and Tim just had to bring their top secret attaché cases along.

As they drove up to the Recital Hall, they found it far different from the deserted hall they had seen just the day before. Heavy traffic plied the streets and men and women dressed in formal attire—tuxedos and gowns—strode eagerly toward the entrance. It was to be the event of the year, and Washington was laying out its red carpet as only it knows how.

"Welcome Timothy Wright, esquire," announced a handsome lighted sign. Concessionaires were having a heyday selling programs and mementos.

As the cousins' limo pulled up to the front entry drop-off zone, the host and valet met them. "Thank you, sir," the host said. "May I ask the name of your party?"

"The Timothy Wright party," the driver replied.

There was an audible hush in the crowd. "Timothy Wright's here," someone whispered. "The poet, the poet–he's here!" said another. Cameras started flashing. "The poet has arrived!"

Straightening their clothing as well as possible, Kimberly, Lindy, Tim, and Jonathan stepped from the long limousine, followed by Robert, Uncle Steve, and Princess Katrina. In the excitement of the moment, no one seemed to notice that Steve was the only one carrying an attaché case.

Amidst much applause, the group was escorted to their special VIP seats in the recital hall. From there, Tim and Kimberly were escorted to the stage. There was a special excitement in the air. *The moment the whole artistic world was waiting for was about to begin!*

CHAPTER 22

The Great Poem Recital

The recital hall's interior was even more majestic than its beautiful stone exterior. Luxurious carpets covered its floors and gold-framed, classical paintings hung on warm walnut walls. High overhead, sparkling, graceful golden chandeliers lit the foyer and stairways.

Tim and Kimberly followed their host to the wings of the stage. The musicians were completing their warm-up in the orchestral pit and the program was about to begin.

"There's a couple here to see you," said their host.

"Mom and Dad!" Tim said excitedly. "You made it!" Tim and Kimberly rushed over and gave their parents hugs.

"Timothy, we're so proud of you," said Mrs. Wright. "But why aren't you dressed in your nice clothes?"

"Sorry, Mom, we lost our luggage and didn't have time to buy new ones," said Kimberly. "A lot has happened since we talked with you. We'll have to explain later."

"Well, Tim, win the audience over with your dazzling smile," said Mrs. Wright encouragingly. "Did you hear that the President is here tonight?"

"Good evening," boomed a voice over the hall's sound system. "Welcome to the POEMNET INTERNATIONAL POET AND WHIZBANGER SOCIETY'S ANNUAL EXTRAVAGANZA. As you know, we have a very special treat tonight."

"Do you remember your poem, dear?" asked his mom.

"Yes, Mom."

"Now, when you get out there, there will be a ton of people, but don't get nervous."

"I'll be fine, Mom," said Tim. "Um...how many people?"

"Ten thousand or so," said his mom. Tim gulped. "You'll do just great, though," continued his mom. "And don't mind the television cameras from all over the world–."

"Mom and Dad," interrupted Kimberly. "Don't you need to be getting to your seats?"

"I wanted to stay to support Tim," said their mom.

"Thanks, Mom," said Kimberly. "I'll coach him. We'll do fine. Please hurry and find your seats before Tim does his part."

"Kim's right, Honey," said their dad. "We'd better hurry."

"Oh, all right. Isn't this exciting, and just think, the President of the United States is here tonight!"

Tim's stomach was beginning to feel a little funny as he watched his parents leave. "Thanks Sis," he said, his voice cracking. "Mom was beginning to get me worried."

Tim and Kimberly watched from the wing of the stage as several people pronounced their award-winning poems. Before they knew it, it was Tim's time to go on stage.

"You can do it," Kimberly encouraged. "Just tell the audience your poem like you told it to me back home, okay?"

"Okay," said Tim with an uncertain grin. "But I hope they don't make me wash the dishes."

"And now," they heard the announcer say, "the moment we have all been waiting for. I am pleased to present to you Mr. PoemNet winner himself, Mr. Timothy Wright, Esquire, Poet-at-large. Let's have a big round of applause for Mr. Timothy Wright!"

Tim peeked from behind the curtain and got his first look at the huge audience.

"Just pretend you're back home in our house," reminded Kimberly.

"Mr. Timothy Wright," announced the host a second time.

Tim walked stiffly toward center stage. The bright spotlights highlighted him every inch of the way. He could feel the sweat starting to bead on his forehead. Reaching the podium, he nervously adjusted the microphone and looked out over the huge concert hall. Through the blinding spotlights, Tim spied thousands of people looking eagerly back at him.

"Good evening," Tim said bravely. "My name is–." He glanced down at his feet. "My name is–." Try as he might, *Tim could not even remember his name!*

CHAPTER 23

Overthrown

Someone in an upper balcony called out, "YAY TIM!"

"Hi Mom," Tim called back with a smile. The audience laughed and broke into applause. The laughter broke the ice, giving Tim a chance to relax a bit and catch his breath. "Folks," he said, "I'd like to introduce you to the greatest parents in the world, Mr. and Mrs. Kevin and Rebecca Wright. Mom and Dad, could you please stand?"

Tim's mom and dad stood and the spotlights picked them out in the VIP section.

"Thanks," said Tim as everyone clapped. The spotlights returned to Tim. Tim glanced back at the program. "I will now recite my poem for you. It's called...***KNIGHT AND DAY.***"

The hall was so silent you could hear a pin drop.

"I saw a knight named Day," Tim began, his voice only cracking once.

"The trees are leaving, April, May.
Airplanes fly, thinking soundly,
Moon defies view, looking roundly."

"Bravo, bravo," shouted someone in the crowd. A thunderous applause burst forth from the audience.

"Ground watch, rooks, many pawns; start sprinklers, water lawns."

Tim had to pause again, for the whole audience had gone crazy, cheering and clapping and hurrahing. He had to wait a whole minute before they had settled down enough for him to continue.

"There, because," said Tim, completing his poem and humbly bowing.

The audience erupted into applause again. People spontaneously stood up all over the theater, giving Tim a huge standing ovation.

"More!" people chanted down from the balconies. "Encore, encore!" shouted others from the main floor.

The master of ceremonies announcer came over and waved his hand for the audience to quiet down. "Ladies and Gentlemen," he proclaimed. "I am sure Master Wright is thrilled with your reception. Perhaps we might persuade him to share with us another of his poems."

Another thunderous applause broke out and only quieted again when Tim stepped back up to the microphone.

"Thank you very much," said Tim. "But I'm afraid I didn't come prepared–."

"Po-em! Po-em!" chanted a large section of the upper balcony. It grew louder. **"Po-em! Po-em!"**

"Okay," said Tim, "wow. Well, maybe I can show you...how I compose. I'm the kind of person who likes to do it right off the top of my head. First, I start with a title. Let's see, how about...THE INCREDIBLE JOURNEY."

You could have heard another pin drop in the recital hall. Everyone leaned forward in anticipation.

"THE INCREDIBLE JOURNEY," Tim began.
"From peak to peak, I climbed all day,
And as I climbed, I'd rock and sway.
I cannot lie, I cannot fib–

I finally reached...the top of the crib!"

The hall was dead silent. There was no laughter, no clapping, no anything. It was as if all the people were frozen in time.

"Didn't the audience get it?" thought Tim, sweat beginning to roll down his sideburns. "It's about a baby," he said self-consciously, "you know, a crib and all that."

Like the trickle before the flood, someone high up in the highest balcony was heard to say, "*profound, profound.*" Everyone burst into applause.

"Thank you, Master Timothy Wright, sir," said the master of ceremonies. "We look forward to hearing much more of your work in the future."

The audience continued to cheer while Tim bowed and then strode over to the wing of the stage to meet Kimberly.

"And now, to present the remainder of the program–," continued the announcer.

"Great job, little brother," Kimberly said when Tim got behind the curtain.

"I don't know about this poet stuff, Kimberly," said Tim, tugging at his shirt collar. "It's really tough out there."

"You did just fine. A lot better than I could have done," said Kimberly, grinning. "Follow me. There's someone who wants to meet you."

Without further explanation, Kimberly led Tim to the top of the VIP section. "We're here to meet the President of the United States of America," announced Kimberly when they arrived at a guarded door.

"Yes, Miss," replied the guard. "Please wait a moment."

Speaking into a radio, the guard said, "I have a young lady and a young man here to meet the President."

"He's expecting them. Send them in."

"Yes sir," replied the guard. He opened the door and let Kimberly and Tim pass.

"The *real* President?" whispered Tim.

"Of course," Kimberly replied with a smile.

Passing through the doorway, the two youths spied several rows of seats in a large room. A thick, bulletproof glass window at the front gave an excellent view of the recital hall stage. A small group of people was standing at the rear of the room in an open area. Princess Katrina and Uncle Steve were among them.

Everyone was enjoying the evening immensely. Everyone, that is, except Veep. He, too, was in the VIP room, but known by a different, more distinguished name. Veep just stood there in the President's bulletproof room, nervously trying to figure out how he was going to get his hands on the attaché case which Colonel Steve Green had just handed over to the President.

Seeing his niece and nephew arrive, Steve Green greeted them and led them over to meet the President. Unbeknownst to Tim, one of his shoelaces was loose. On the way to meet the President, he tripped on the lace and stumbled into an important-looking man in a dark suit, knocking him down. To his horror, Tim discovered his accidental victim was none other than the Vice President of the United States.

"I'm sorry," Tim said apologetically as he got up off the Vice President. "I didn't mean to–."

"Clumsy oaf," rebuked the Vice President, sitting up. "No wonder there's so much delinquency in America today."

"I'm sure my brother didn't mean to, sir," Kimberly said, standing up for Tim.

"Don't touch me," said the Vice President. "And I don't like your poetry, either."

"Nice necktie," Tim said to the Vice President, ignoring his remarks. Tim's eyes settled on the man's tie tack. It was a round circle with a golden sprig of broccoli in the middle. "Hey," said Tim aloud. "Mr. Vice President, sir, what are you doing with the Broccoli Brigade symbol? I thought only the terrorists wore...wait a minute, you're Veep, aren't you! Kimberly, he's VEEP!"

In a sudden rage, the Vice President shoved Kimberly and Tim aside, snatched the attaché case from the President's hand, and ran from the room.

Uncle Steve dashed after him and shouted, "Stop that traitor!"

CHAPTER 24

Surprise Attack

The security around the U.S. President that night had been set up to protect him from the outside, not from within. The Vice President–Veep–cleared the security force and dashed up to the Recital Hall roof. There, he leapt aboard an awaiting helicopter and was whisked away.

Devastated by the Vice President's betrayal, the President painfully ordered an all-out pursuit and investigation. The President and his aides immediately excused themselves, and Princess Katrina and the cousins were ushered from the room. U.S. Special Forces scoured Washington, D.C., and its environs, but to no avail. The Vice President's plans had been too cleverly laid. He had changed over to a supersonic plane and was now out of the country. The mission which Princess Katrina, Uncle Steve, and the cousins had fought so hard to accomplish was now suddenly turned upside-down. The vital attaché case would soon be in the hands of America's worst enemies!

"Our own Vice President a traitor," said Kimberly, glancing over at Tim.

"Don't look at me," replied Tim. "I didn't mean to trip. Me and my untied shoes."

"You did just fine, Tim," said Uncle Steve as they walked down the hallway from the president's room. "You revealed the identity of the biggest traitor to our country; that scummy Veep has been selling us all out."

"Yeah, but he got away, Uncle Steve," Tim said, downcast.

Uncle Steve put his arm around Tim's shoulder. "Don't take it too hard, Tim. You've done far more than you think in helping America, you will see."

"Really?" said Tim, perking up a bit.

"Really," answered Uncle Steve with a smile. "That broccoli symbol you noticed does not stand for a vegetable. It represents the terrorists' intent to destroy anyone in their way through a fiery mushroom, the nuclear bomb."

"Wow," said Tim and Kimberly at the same time.

"Well, I for one, am starving," said Steve Green. "What do you say we go and find something to eat?"

"Mr. Green?" Princess Katrina asked, studying Steve's cheerful face. "How can you think of eating at a time like this?"

"Princess, thanks to the Wright cousins, you and I are free," replied Steve. "I think that deserves a celebration. Tim, let's treat the princess to some good ol' American food."

"Now you're talking," said Tim with relish in his voice. "Princess Katrina, how about a big, juicy American hamburger."

Turning a corner, the small group was joined in the hallway by Mr. and Mrs. Wright, Jonathan, Lindy, Robert, *and* great Aunt Opal.

"Dinner is an excellent idea," said great Aunt Opal. "It will cheer everyone up. There's nothing like a good, family sit-down meal to brighten your day. I propose the Hamburger Delight restaurant I saw earlier down the street."

Before they knew it, they were ordering custom burgers at Hamburger Delight and hearing about Aunt Opal's adventures. It was a busy night for the restaurant, so the group had to be divided into two groups, seated in adjacent booths.

Tim's parents and Aunt Opal were seated at one table, and Steve, Princess Katrina, and the cousins were at the other. Near the end of their meal, Aunt Opal began to fidget. "Ouch," she said, rubbing her ear.

"What's wrong, Aunt Opal?" asked Lindy from the adjacent booth.

"Oh, dearie me," she said, "my hearing aid is acting up again. It keeps making loud noises. Lindy, do you think you could have your brother fix it again?"

"Sure," said Lindy. "Robert can fix anything. I'll give it to him."

Aunt Opal slipped out her hearing aid and Lindy passed it over to Robert. Robert soon had a small access cover pulled off. "Let's see," he said, holding the hearing aid to his ear and adjusting the volume. "The switch doesn't seem to be–hey, wait a minute, what's this?"

Robert turned up the volume and cupped a spoon around it so all at his table could hear. "Hey guys, listen to this," he said. "It sounds like a phone call."

"Yes, Mr. American President, sir," a man was saying in a mocking voice. "I am no longer your inferior–."

"That sounds like the Vice President," said Uncle Steve. "What are you guys picking up?"

Lindy, Kimberly, Katrina, Tim and Jonathan all leaned closer.

"You *traitor*," said a second voice. "How can you betray America like this?"

Uncle Steve was doubly concerned and said, "That's the President's voice. How are you guys getting that? He always talks on a *secure* line."

"Aunt Opal listens to the most interesting things," said Lindy, grinning.

"Listen," said Robert. "There's more."

"I have been promised your position, Mr. President," said the Vice President. "They know my loyalty. I have given them the top secret attaché case."

"How could you," said the President. "You know that will leave America defenseless!"

"Correct," said a new voice.

"That's Skunkk," Uncle Steve said with disgust. "Boy! Get a high position so you can peddle your power and help your bad guy friends. Veep and Skunkk, what a bunch of scummy gadiantons!"

Skunkk continued in cruel delight, "Mr. past-President of America, your old Vice President and I will now open the Straunsee attaché case here in my bombproof bunker. I hold in my hands the American *football,* the presidential control of all America's vast nuclear arsenal and anti-missile systems. With this, we will paralyze America's defense systems. I have been assigned the–what's the correct word?–the *privilege* of bringing America to her knees. We, your former Vice President and I, will have the delightful task of turning you and the rest of America into slaves. You will be in *my* power. Ha-ha-ha," he laughed evilly. "I must admit that I shall enjoy seeing you in chains."

"You wouldn't dare," said the President. "We'll fight you to our last drop of blood."

"As you wish," Skunkk replied. "And now for the attaché case. Mr. Vice President, if you will assist me."

"Certainly," replied the Vice President gleefully.

Clicking the locks open, the two men eagerly lifted the lid. There was a sudden hissing sound, like the sound of someone using a fire extinguisher.

"Puey," said the Vice President. "What did they put in this?"

"Double puey," replied Skunkk. "I don't know, but it's definitely not–."

There was a loud ***Pop!***

"What's the meaning of this, Veep?" Skunkk said angrily.

Green fumes began billowing from the attaché case as the two men fought to close it. ***Poomph!*** Another bomb went off, filling the room with greenish-white smoke.

"Aaugh!" shrieked Skunkk. "Veep, you've bungled your last–phewie, this stuff stinks–job. I'll send you to the slave mines for this!"

"What's going on?" asked Kimberly.

"Don't look at me," said Jonathan. "I'm just the driver."

"Tim?" said Kimberly.

"I didn't do anything," Tim replied. "But it sounds like one of our secret weapons, all right. But how?"

All eyes at the table turned to Robert, who was struggling to keep a straight face. "All right, all right," he said, "I have a confession to make. Uncle Steve and I switched the contents of our attaché cases before we got out of the armored car. Veep got some of our Broccoli Bombs."

"Good job," said Jonathan, giving Robert a high-five.

"You know," said Uncle Steve, "you guys still haven't told me how you got the armored car."

"You mean our new SUV?" said Robert.

"The one with the environmentally-friendly, forest green camouflage job?" Lindy added.

"Right," said Uncle Steve. "You guys aren't thinking about becoming secret agents or something, are you?"

"Us, secret agents?" said Tim. "Well–." Kimberly elbowed him to be quiet.

"Actually, it's just our new set of wheels," Robert replied. "We're going to buy it so we can take it home."

Uncle Steve laughed. "Even if you could," he said, "do you know how much something like that costs?"

"It's a pre-owned, used vehicle," Lindy replied thoughtfully, crunching the numbers. "So probably about $200,000."

"Right," said Uncle Steve. "And where would you guys get that kind of money?" He paused, looking around at each of the grinning cousins. "All right you guys, out with it," he said. "What's so funny?"

CHAPTER 25

A Happy Ending?

After dinner, everyone climbed into the stretched limousine. Uncle Steve directed the chauffer to drive to the White House. He was anxious to meet with the President and complete his mission.

Security was heightened around the White House. The adjacent streets had roadblocks with checkpoints established. It took some real explaining and a phone call to the President, but the limousine with its passengers was finally allowed to proceed.

At the driveway entrance, Colonel Steve Green got out and strode quickly to the White House, carrying a top secret attaché case. A guard posted there let him pass and he was ushered in to see the President.

Twenty minutes later, Uncle Steve emerged from the White House, minus the attaché case.

"Good news, Mr. Green?" asked the princess.

"Wonderful news," replied Steve. "We have successfully done what we set out to do. The attaché is safely in the proper hands."

"That is well," said Katrina with a relieved smile.

Steve climbed aboard the limousine. "Chauffeur," he called, "Please take us to the Golden Chariot Hotel. Thanks to the President of the United States, we can have the best rooms in the house. And boy, am I looking forward to a good night's sleep!"

"Yes sir," replied the chauffer.

Katrina was given a beautiful suite. She requested the girls stay in the suite's adjoining room and they very happily agreed. Jonathan bunked with Tim and Robert. Mr. and Mrs. Wright got their own room, and great Aunt Opal and Steve each got their own rooms, too. An armed guard was posted outside each of the five rooms.

The next morning, the world was a-buzz with new headlines:

SHOCKING BETRAYAL! AMERICA'S VP A MODERN BENEDICT ARNOLD!

AMERICAN PRESIDENT WARNS: BEWARE OF TERRORISTS IN SHEEP'S CLOTHING!

ZERGBY RACCOONS WIN THE PENNANT!

POEMNET SUPERSTAR RECITES NEW SMASH POEM!

AWESOME "*INCREDIBLE JOURNEY*" PACKS 1-2 PUNCH WHILE THOUSANDS REJOICE– REMEMBERING THEIR BABYHOOD!

At 9am, the cousins' group met in Princess Katrina's suite for a delicious breakfast. The large rooms were bright and cheery with huge plate glass windows, affording an excellent view of the Washington skyline.

"This is a breakfast fit for a king!" said Tim as he eagerly sat down to eat.

"The chef has done well," said Katrina.

After breakfast, great Aunt Opal excused herself. When she returned, she was carrying two colorfully-wrapped presents. "I brought you all milk chocolates from England," she announced.

"Really?" said Tim, eagerly taking one of the boxes and opening it.

"Aunt Opal, you shouldn't have," said Mrs. Wright.

"It's okay, Mom," Tim said. "They look great."

"Chocolates? Oooo," said Kimberly, eagerly opening the second box.

"What do you kids say?" said Mr. Wright.

"Thank you, Aunt Opal," chorused the cousins. The room was now filled with the sweet aroma of rich milk chocolate.

Tim took two of the treats and popped them into his mouth. "Mmmm, they're great," he said, relishing their smooth, soft texture as he chewed. "These are almost as good as those chocolates Aunt Opal brought back for us from Switzerland last year."

The more Tim chewed, the more the chocolates began to take on an unusual flavor. Kimberly kindly passed the treats around to the others in the room.

"Unusual shape," said Robert, holding up one of the chocolates between his thumb and index finger. "They kind of look like little mushrooms."

"Not mushrooms," replied Aunt Opal enthusiastically. "They're actually chocolate-coated broccoli spears. And they're *so good* for you."

Tim gagged. "Chocolate-covered what?" he said, accidentally swallowing one. He got a distressed look on his face like he'd just been poisoned.

"They're from the *Bucolic Broccoli Buffet* in London," said great Aunt Opal. "And they're organic."

"*Broccoli Buffet?*" said Tim, suddenly clamping his hand over his mouth. "I think I'm gonna be sick."

"Tim, honey dear," said Aunt Opal. "Aren't they wonderful? I wish *everybody* could have some."

"Yeah, I do to. In fact, they can have mine," said Tim, turning green and nearly keeling over.

That afternoon, the Wright cousins group went with Princess Katrina to the airport. A private jet airplane had been chartered to take her home.

"Goodbye," said each of the cousins in turn as they hugged her. All except Tim, and he was pretending to be busy tying his shoelaces.

"Tim," said Katrina. "I must go. But before I go, I must give you the largest hug of all, because it was you who discovered me first."

Tim turned to bolt but Robert stopped him.

"Robert," protested Tim, "what are you doing? She's gonna hug me."

"Sorry, old buddy," Robert whispered with a grin. "Stiff upper lip, Tim. You've got to take it like a man."

Tim turned around. Princess Katrina caught him and hugged him tight. "Thank you," she said gratefully.

"Well what do you say, Tim?" said Mrs. Wright.

"I can't breathe," Tim replied, his face turning pink with embarrassment. "But you're welcome, Katrina."

Katrina let go of Tim, stepped back, and grinned. "Maybe you and my younger sister, Maria, could write to each other," she suggested.

Tim's face turned even more pink. Katrina, a bit of a tease herself, was enjoying the moment. She glanced around at all the Wright cousins. "Thank you again, each and every one of you," she said. "I must be going."

Princess Katrina waved good-bye to the group and left for

her plane.

"Write her younger sister? Whew," said Tim, breathing a sigh of relief when Katrina was gone, "thank goodness she didn't get my email address."

"Oh, she's got it," mentioned Kimberly with a smile. "Last night, Lindy and I gave her all of our emails."

"That's way no fair," replied Tim. "That's top secret information on a need-to-know basis only."

"What can I say," Kimberly smiled back, "she *needed* to know." The rest of the cousins laughed.

For the next two days, the Wright Cousins' group played tourist. They saw the Washington, Lincoln, and Jefferson Memorials. They visited the Capitol building and the Library of Congress. They also saw Mount Vernon and Arlington House. And of course, everywhere they went, Aunt Opal played tour guide and often commented on how much better Tim was doing at keeping his shoes tied properly.

On their last night in Washington, Robert and Tim were alone in their room, packing. Suddenly, there was a loud knock on their door. When Tim opened it, he saw two men in dark suits standing there.

"Is Robert Wright here?" asked one of the men.

"Yes," said Tim.

"Good," said the man, flipping open his billfold to show Tim a shiny metal badge. "I'm Agent Morris and this is Agent Sharp. We're with the FBI."

Tim studied Morris' badge. "FBI? Um—yeah, well, Robert's the one you need to talk to." Tim showed the men in and he and Robert nervously introduced themselves.

"Is there something wrong, sir?" asked Robert.

"Let's just say we need you to answer a few questions for us," replied Morris.

"Oh," gulped Robert and Tim at the same time.

"In fact," continued Agent Morris, "we're here representing several U.S. Government agencies: the FBI, the CIA, the Department of Defense, the SIA, and the Treasury, to name a few."

"Oh," said Robert, glancing at Tim, "that's a few."

"It would seem that we have some common friends," said Agent Morris.

"We do?" asked Tim.

"Yes, and we need you to get a message to them."

"Who?" Robert asked.

Agent Morris glanced warily around the room and whispered, "You know, *them.*"

"Them?" said Robert.

"Yes. A computer glitch has caused us to lose contact with two of our top people. We understand you guys can get in touch with them. We need you to tell special agents Kimosoggy and Toronto something."

Robert and Tim glanced at each other.

"Tell them," continued Agent Morris, "Delta Code Red."

"Code Red?" asked Robert.

"Yes. *Delta* Code Red. Emergency Plan C-42. Download immediately."

"Wow," said Robert.

"Exactly," said Morris. "And tell them to use *more* money this time. We don't want our budget to be cut. Well, come on, Sharp, we'd better get going."

Robert and Tim escorted the two FBI agents to the door. Just as Robert was closing it, he overheard Agent Morris comment to his companion, "Can you imagine that, Clark? Kimosoggy and Toronto are America's top two agents, and yet they use those poor little innocent kids as fronts."

"Yes, the nerve of some people," Agent Clark replied. "No wonder the President's letting those kids and their relatives fly home on Air Force One for free."

A brief time later, there was another knock at Robert and Tim's door. This time it was Lindy and she had a pile of newspaper clippings with her. "Robert and Tim," she said, "can you believe these headlines?"

> **"PRINCESS KATRINA FOUND ALIVE IN WASHINGTON, D.C.! MIRACULOUSLY ESCAPES KIDNAPPING!**
>
> **HOLLYWOOD SEEKS STORY RIGHTS FOR MOVIE..."**

"And look what I pulled off the Internet," continued Lindy.

> *The National Conspirer* says, **"PRINCESS BROUGHT TO U.S. ABOARD FLYING SAUCER FROM ALPHA CENTAURI."**
>
> **"A HAPPY ENDING!"** declared *The New York Rhymes.*

"Happy ending?" said Robert. "What's this happy ending stuff?"

"Well Robert," said Lindy. "This *is* the end of the story, you know."

"What? It can't be. Lindy, we've still got to tell about how we..."

"Look, you two, we caught all the bad guys, right?"

"Right," said Robert and Tim, nodding in agreement.

"And we bought the armored car and we're having it shipped home, right?"

"Well, yes, disguised as a motor home," said Robert.

"And we rescued Uncle Steve and Princess Katrina, and Princess Katrina is on her way home, right?"

"Yes," replied both boys.

"Well then," said Lindy. "This must be the end."

"But Lindy," Robert protested. "What about our plans to–."

"Hush," said Lindy. "Do you want to spoil what happens in our next adventure?"

"You mean we can't even mention about our invitation to see the Sea M-O-N-S-T-R-E?" asked Tim.

"That's Sea *M-O-N-S-T-E-R*," said Lindy, shaking her head. "And no, not a single word!"

"I protest!" said Robert. "The citizens of America have a right to know!"

"But it's TOP SECRET," said Lindy.

"I know what we can do," said Robert with a smile. "We'll write an open letter to the President and send it to a newspaper."

"And the Internet," said Tim.

"Yes," said Robert. "And it'll go something like this...

"To whom it may concern and the President of the United States of America:

We, Kimosoggy and Toronto, are good and patriotic Americans. We're here to help make sure that America survives. We laugh at danger."

"That's good," said Tim. "I like that *laugh* part."

"We fear no bad guys," Robert continued.

"Of course not," said Tim.

"We catch crooks and we straight-jacket terrorists!"

"That's telling them," said Tim.

"And we're *not* afraid of Broccoli–."

"Well, I wouldn't go that far," said Tim.

"We're two sharp cookies–."

"And we're humble, too," added Tim.

"Right," said Robert. "And when we're done, we'll sign it 'anonymous' because we don't want anybody to know who we are."

"Robert, your watch is beeping," said Tim.

"You know," said Lindy as Robert checked his watch. "I think I like *The New York Rhymes* headline the best."

"Which one?" said Robert and Tim at the same time.

"The one that talks about **'A HAPPY ENDING.'** But I think in our case, I'd call it **'A VERY HAPPY ENDING,'** wouldn't you?"

Please write a review

Authors love hearing from their readers!

Please let Greg Smith know what you thought about *Secret Agents Don't Like Broccoli* by leaving a short review on Amazon or your other preferred online store. If you are under age 13, please ask an adult to help you. Your review will help other people find this fun and exciting new adventure.

Thank you!

Top tip: be sure not to give away any of the story's secrets!

About the Author

Greg exploring the bottom of the mine shaft seen in the book video trailer for *The Treasure of the Lost Mine*. You can watch the book video trailer for *Secret Agents Don't Like Broccoli* at the author's website, GregoryOSmith.com.

Gregory O. Smith loves life! All of Greg's books are family friendly. He grew up in a family of four boys that rode horses, explored Old West gold mining ghost towns, and got to help drive an army tank across the Southern California desert in search of a crashed airplane!

Hamburgers are his all-time favorite food! (Hold the tomatoes and pickles, please.) Boysenberry pie topped with homemade vanilla ice cream is a close second. His current hobby is detective-like family history research.

Greg and his wife have raised five children and he now enjoys playing with his wonderful grandkids. He has been a Junior High School teacher and lived to tell about it. He has also been a water well driller, game and toy manufacturer, army mule mechanic, gold miner, railroad engineer, and living history adventure tour guide. (Think: dressing up as a Pilgrim, General George Washington, a wily Redcoat, or a California Gold Rush miner. Way too much fun!)

Greg's design and engineering background enables him to build things people can enjoy such as obstacle courses, waterwheels and ride-on railroads. His books are also fun filled, technically accurate, and STEM–Science, Technology, Engineering, and Math–supportive. Now, if he could just figure out how Tim Wright keeps drawing on his brand new book covers.

Greg likes visiting with his readers and hearing about their favorite characters and events in the books. To see the fun video trailers for the books and learn about the latest Wright cousin adventures, please visit **GregoryOSmith.com** today!

ALSO BY GREGORY O. SMITH

The Wright Cousin Adventures –

Get the complete set!

1 **The Treasure of the Lost Mine**—Meet the five Wright cousins in their first big mystery together. I mean, what could be more fun than a treasure hunt with five crazy, daring, ingenious, funny and determined teenagers, right? The adventure grows as the cousins run headlong into vanishing trains, trap doors, haunted gold mines and surprises at every turn!

2 **Desert Jeepers**—The five Wright cousins are having a blast 4-wheeling in the desert as they look for a long-lost Spanish treasure ship. And who wouldn't? There's so much to see! Palm trees, hidden treasure, UFO's, vanishing stagecoaches, incredible hot sauce, missing pilots. Wait! What?!

3 **The Secret of the Lost City**—A mysterious map holds the key to the location of an ancient treasure city. When the Wright cousins set out on horseback to find it, they run

headlong into desert flash floods, treacherous passages, and formidable foes. Saddle up for thrilling discoveries and the cousins' wacky sense of humor in this grand Western adventure!

4 **The Case of the Missing Princess**—The Wright cousins are helping to restore a stone fort from the American Revolution. They expect hard work, but find more—secret passages, pirates, dangerous waterfalls, a new girl with a fondness for swordplay. Join the cousins as they try to unravel this puzzling new mystery!

5 **Secret Agents Don't Like Broccoli**—The spy world will never be the same! Teenage cousins Robert and Tim Wright accidentally become America's top two secret agents—the notorious KIMOSOGGY and TORONTO. Their mission: rescue the beautiful Princess Katrina Straunsee and the mysterious, all-important Straunsee attaché case. They must not fail, for the future of America is in their hands. Get set for top secret fun and adventure as the Wright cousins outsmart the entire spy world—we hope!

6 **The Great Submarine Adventure**—The five Wright cousins have a submarine and they know how to use it! But the deeper they go, the more mysterious Lake Pinecone becomes. Something is wrecking boats on the lake and it's downright scary. Will they find the secret before it's too late? It's "up periscope" and "man the torpedoes" as the fun-loving Wright cousins dive into this exciting new adventure!

7 **Take to the Skies**—The Wright cousins are using their World War 2 seaplane to solve a puzzling mystery, but someone keeps sabotaging their efforts. Then a sudden lightning storm moves in and the local mountains erupt into

flames. The cousins must fly into action to rescue their friends. Will their seaplane hold together long enough to help them survive the raging forest fires? Join the Wright cousins in this thrilling new adventure!

8 **The Wright Cousins Fly Again**—Secret bases, missing airplanes, and an unsolved World War 2 mystery are keeping the Wright cousins busy. Then the cousins discover a secret lurking deep in Lake Pinecone that is far more dangerous than they ever expected. Will all their carefully made plans be wrecked? Will they survive? You'd better have a life preserver and parachute ready for this fun and exciting new adventure!

9 **Reach for the Stars**—3-2-1-Blastoff! The Wright cousins are out of this world and so is the fun. Join the cousins as they travel into space aboard the new Stellar Spaceplane. Enjoy zero gravity and the incredible views. But what about those space aliens Tim keeps seeing? The Wrights soon discover there really is something out there and it's really scary. The cousins must pull together—with help from family and friends back on earth—if they are to survive. It's what family and friendship is all about. Get ready for fun and adventure as the Wright cousins *REACH FOR THE STARS!*

10 **The Sword of Sutherlee**—These are dangerous times in the kingdom of Gütenberg. King Straunsee and his daughters have been made prisoners in their own castle. The five Wright cousins rush in to help. With secret passages and swords in hand, the cousins must scramble to rescue their friends and the kingdom. Can they do it? Find out in this fun and exciting new adventure!

11 **The Secret of Trifid Castle**—A redirected airline flight leads the Wright cousins back into adventure: mysterious

luggage, racing rental cars, cool spy gear, secret bunkers, and menacing foes. Lives hang in the balance. Who can they trust? Join the Wright cousins on a secret mission in this fun, daring, and exciting new adventure!

12 **The Clue in the Missing Plane**— A cold war is about to turn hot in the Kingdom of Gütenberg. Snowstorms, jagged mountains, enemy soldiers. Can the Wright cousins discover a top secret clue before they become prisoners? Dive in with the Wright cousins in this thrilling new adventure!

Additional Books by Gregory O. Smith

The Hat, George Washington, and Me!—When a mysterious package arrives in the mail with only a tricorn hat and a playset inside, fourteen-year-old Daniel, of course, tries on the hat. Now he's in for it because the hat won't come off! Daniel suddenly finds bullies at every turn, redcoats pounding on the school room door, and a patriot in his cereal box! It's modern-day Millford—a town that is not on the map—and time is running out. Will Daniel and his friend, Rebecca, solve the mystery of the hat before it's too late?

Rheebakken 2: Last Stand for Freedom—The fate of the Free World is at stake. Alpha Command super-pilot Eric Brown has already had one airplane shot-out from under him. He's in no mood to let it happen again. Join Eric Brown, King Straunsee, and stubborn Princess Allesandra as they fight to keep freedom alive. Can they do it? This fast-paced, exciting new adventure is enjoyed by children *and* adults alike!

Strength of the Mountains—Balloon camping? The morning arrives. The balloon is filled. An unexpected storm strikes. Matt, all alone, is swept off into the wilderness in an unfinished balloon. Totally lost, what will he find? How will he survive? Will he ever make it home again? It's an exciting story of wilderness survival and growing friendships. Join the adventure!

Get the complete set!

Please tell your family and friends about these fun and exciting new adventures so they can enjoy them too!

Printed in Great Britain
by Amazon